TIME TRAITOR

American Epochs: Volume I

By Todd McClimans

Northampton House Press

TIME TRAITOR. Copyright 2014 by Todd McClimans. All rights reserved, including the right to reproduce this book, or portions thereof, in any form.

Cover design by Tim Ogline.

First Northampton House Press edition, 2014. ISBN 978-1-937997-36-6.

www.northampton-house.com

10   9   8   7   6   5   4   3   2

TIME TRAITOR

ONE

Kristi Connors slipped through the dim, empty halls of George Washington Prep in a gray hoodie, black socks, and no shoes. She peeked around corners and hugged the lockers like a ninja, staying out of the orange circles of security lights dotting the ceilings in each hall.

She turned down the intermediate hall, then jumped back and shrank into a crevice between lockers. One hand yanked the strings hanging from the hoodie, closing the hood to a slit over her eyes. She held her breath.

A squeaking sound came first, like a loose wheel of a cart. Then shuffling boots. Finally a white haired man in a blue jumpsuit pushed a dry mop around the corner. Headphone cords dangled from his bobbing head and he whistled softly through a bushy mustache. He trundled past without looking her way, turned down an adjoining hallway.

When the squeaking faded, Kristi emerged and slid down the lockers to the cove of sixth grade classrooms. She stopped before a door with darkened, smoky glass. *Dr. Arnold* was inscribed on the brass nameplate screwed into the frame. She picked the lock with two hairpins and stole in. Pulling back the hood, she revealed her smooth, light chocolate-hued skin and zigzagging black braids that hung to the nape of her neck.

Leaving the flashlight in her pocket, she felt her way through the dim room to the teacher's desk. Easing the center drawer open, she tied a Pull-Snap between drawer and desk, and closed it again, careful not to disturb any of the papers on the

1

desktop. Then she knelt and used a tiny screwdriver to remove all the screws from the back wheels of the chair.

With a grin, she pulled her hood back up and breezed out.

***

Ty Jordan descended the metal steps of the Jefferson boys' dormitory, treading carefully so the sound of his footfalls wouldn't echo up the narrow stairwell. He followed his long shadow past the main level, into the basement. The air turned musty, heavy with mold and laundry detergent. When he flipped the switch, the fluorescents in the low ceiling flickered, then hummed to life, illuminating a wall of washing machines facing a wall of dryers with a thin metal drain splitting the concrete floor between them. A small rectangular window in the opposite wall showed a bleaching sky, the faint beginnings of dawn. He guessed he had thirty minutes before the others were up.

He tossed his book sack between two dryers, then thumbed quarters into the coin slots and fired them up empty. When low, surf-like drones filled the room, he squeezed between the dryers and sat with his back against the block wall. He dug his history book out and opened it across his thighs.

Causes of the Revolutionary War:
The American colonists, increasingly agitated at what they deemed excessive and unfair taxes imposed by the King and Parliament, took to the streets in protest, boycotted British goods, and eventually engaged in open rebellion. Parliament responded with a series of—

DONG

Ty flinched at the noise, which sounded like a sledgehammer hitting the Liberty Bell. A round, grinning face leaned over the dryer.

"Mornin', Froggy."

Jeffrey Sampson. The ogre-sized boy stepped into the gap. He was big, almost six feet, with a dark peach-fuzz mustache and pimpled face, looking more ninth grader than sixth.

"You hidin' from us, Frog-boy?" Jeffrey jeered. Two smaller boys stepped up behind him, like tiny fish hoping for scraps from a Great White's kill.

"No," Ty lied and closed his book, keeping a thumb between the pages. But, like every morning, he'd gotten up before the dorm parents knocked, showered quickly, and wolfed down breakfast when only the cooks were in the dining hall. He *was* hiding out, trying to finish homework before classes started.

"So wha'cha *reading*, Froggy?"

"I'm from England, *not* France," Ty muttered.

"Who cares, Frog-face?" The bully ripped the book from him, leaving Ty holding two torn pages.

"Give it back!" Ty pulled himself up. The top of his head barely reached Jeffrey's chest.

"Calm down, Frog-o. I'm just messin' around." He laid a meaty hand on Ty's forehead and pushed him back down. The cronies cackled like hyenas. Jeffrey opened the book and his grin widened. "*The Revolutionary War*? Ha! Plannin' a revolt with your frog-pond friends?" He looked back at the hyenas, tore a handful of pages out, then *tsked*. "Boy, Crazy Arnold's gonna flip when he finds out Frog-butt ripped his *American* history book." He tossed torn pages over one shoulder and dropped the book back onto Ty's lap. "See ya later, Froggy." They clunked up the stairs, snorting laughs echoing down the stairwell.

Ty gathered the scattered pages and stuffed them between the covers. Dr. Arnold, his history teacher, *was* going to be mad, probably make him pay for it. But Ty had used his last two quarters on the dryer, and there was no way his mom's husband was going to shell out the cash. So he'd probably end up in detention.

He sighed and dropped the defaced book into his bag. Time for a new hiding spot. The laundry room had worked well for almost a week, but Jeffrey always seemed to find him, like he had some weird bully sixth sense.

Ty clomped up the steps and out of the dorm's front door, into a graying morning. Rubbing the goose-pimples on his forearms, he trudged across the quad toward the school.

He'd been at George Washington Prep for two months and couldn't imagine a worse place on Earth. His classmates were the spoiled sons and daughters of lawyers, doctors, and politicians who did their best to prove he didn't belong. Jeffrey and his posse intimidated the other students so well that no one would even sit next to him at meals. The trio stole or ruined his homework whenever they could get their hands on it. Ty couldn't even take a shower without worrying his clothes and towel would be dunked in the toilet.

But, as horrible as it was, GW Prep still came in a distant second in terms of the worst things to ever happen to him.

Just six months earlier, his mom had been diagnosed with a rare brain cancer. She'd died within a month.

Ty sighed and climbed the long concrete steps to the school building. As he reached for the front door, it flew open and hit his chest. He staggered back and a flash of gray zoomed past, took three steps toward the stairs, then stopped and turned back slowly. A pretty, dark face looked out from under a hood, brown eyes wide, startled.

"Sorry," the girl mumbled, then took off again, racing down the steps and across the quad.

Kristi Connors, a girl in a few of his classes. One of the better-known students in school, but for all the wrong reasons. Rumor had it the principal kept her picture stuck to a dartboard on the back of his office door. Some kids said her father had donated the money to build a new library just to keep her from getting kicked out. She'd never been mean to Ty, but not friendly either. In fact, that half-hearted apology was the first time she'd actually spoken to him.

So what had she been doing in the school so early? She was always *late* to class. He pulled the door open, deciding he was better off not knowing. The hallway lights flashed on as he entered. He went straight to the library, grabbed a roll of book tape from the counter, and began to piece his history book back together.

***

Kristi rushed into first period class and looked toward the teacher's desk. No Dr. Arnold. The chair and desktop were as she'd left them. Perfect. She glanced up at the clock: 8:05. She'd had enough time to run back to her dorm, dump her sweats and don her uniform, khaki pants and red polo, and get back to class. Early enough to catch the fireworks, but late enough for a classroom full of witnesses to provide her alibi.

As usual, the boys were belching, slugging each other, and throwing paper wads at the English kid. The girls were sitting in a circle of desks chattering like YouTube divas, checking hair and make-up, giggling, staring into compact mirrors. She rolled her eyes. Giggling made her sick.

She scanned for an open desk and locked eyes with the English kid, Ty, she thought his name was. He was smaller than the other boys, timid, almost mousy, as if he'd jump out of his skin if she said 'boo'. But a shiver ran up her spine. He'd seen her that morning. If he snitched, she was toast. She scowled a warning and he looked away. But the only open desk was next to him, so she went over and plopped down.

Like Old Faithful, the clock flashed 8:09 and Dr. Arnold stumbled in, clutching a stack of notebooks and binders to his chest. He looked like a nerdy Mr. Clean, tall and skinny with a shiny, bald head and wrinkled lab coat, complete with plastic pocket protector.

"Quiet down, hooligans." He kicked down the aisle through sprawled legs, dumped his things on the desk and turned, curling his lip as if the classroom was filled with giant slugs.

The roaming boys snickered and slouched off into seats. Dr. Arnold reached for the desk drawer. Kristi leaned forward, holding her breath, but his hand angled off at the last second, picked a marker from a stack of papers, then squeaked across the whiteboard: seventy pages of reading, three worksheets, two essays. Some of the boys groaned, but Arnold glared lasers and they quieted, knowing not to press it. Making Crazy Arnold mad meant triple homework.

Her knee bounced—if only they knew.

"You have fifty minutes," Arnold grumbled and sat. Kristi tensed, but the loosened wheel held. He rifled through papers, frowned, and then—he pulled the middle drawer open.

POP!

Arnold jumped as a plume of blue smoke billowed out. The chair dropped from under him and he pitched back, shrieking like a girl who's seen a hairy spider in the bathtub. His flailing legs sent the whole desk crashing to its face and papers, notebooks, and markers went flying.

A shocked silence stilled the room. The eyes and mouths of Kristi's classmates hung open. No one giggled. No one even breathed.

Dr. Arnold scrambled to his feet. The dissipating smoke looked as if it was streaming from his ears. His red face swelled like an over-inflated birthday balloon. A purple vein on his temple pulsed. Spittle sprayed from his flapping lips as he sputtered angry gibberish.

Kristi bit her lip until she tasted blood. *Don't laugh! Don't laugh!* Out of the corner of one eye, she saw the English kid sink lower in his chair.

"WHO DID THAT?" Arnold stomped a foot. He glared down the rows at every face until he got to Kristi. "*Connors!*"

She folded her hands and smiled like a saint. "Who, me?"

He raced down the aisle, skidded to a stop beside her, and lowered his face close enough for her to smell bitter coffee breath. "I *know* it was you!"

She returned the glare. "But I *just* got here. Ask anybody."

He slapped her desk and turned. "Anyone see Connors here before class? Fifty extra points on the midterm to the one who rats her out."

From the corner of her eye, she saw Ty duck his head, shift in his seat. She readied a hand to sink nails into his bare arm if he opened his mouth.

"A hundred points!" Arnold spat.

She almost cringed at that. A hundred bonus points meant an easy A. It meant no studying for the two-hour test. Heck, that was almost enough to make her turn *herself* in.

But everyone stayed quiet. Ty looked down at his desk and kept his mouth closed.

After a few seconds, she crossed her arms and smirked. "See? I told you! But don't worry. You can't have many enemies, Dr. Arnold. You'll figure it out in no time."

He gritted his teeth, yanked her out of the seat by one arm, then dragged her into the hallway.

"Get off me!" she shouted, bracing her feet.

But he tightened his grip and pulled her down the hall. When they slammed through the office door, the secretary, Ms. Prichart, flinched, sloshing tea onto her ruffled blouse.

"Where's Mr. Cartwright?" Arnold demanded.

"I'm sorry, Dr. Arnold." Ms. Prichart grabbed a tissue, dabbed at the stain. "Mr. Cartwright's in a meeting with the dean, so—"

"Good!" He pulled Kristi past the desk and pushed the principal's door open without knocking. Mr. Cartwright and Dr. Marks were sitting in the leather chairs in front of Cartwright's desk.

"Something has to be done about this girl!" Arnold yanked her arm up.

Mr. Cartwright frowned. "We're in a meeting, Xavier. Come back in—"

"She blew up my desk!" he shouted.

"I did NOT!" She jerked her arm away and stomped a foot. "He's freaking crazy!"

Cartwright pushed little round glasses up from the tip of his stubby nose and stood. The man was short and plump with a ring of ash-gray hair circling a bald pate. Like the students, he wore the school colors, a bright red polo and khaki pants that hung below his round belly. If he'd been wearing a pointy hat, he'd have looked more like the ceramic gnome in Kristi's grandmother's garden than the principal of one the most expensive prep schools in the country.

"Have a seat, Ms. Connors," Mr. Cartwright said.

She groaned and plopped onto the couch. "Whatever."

The dean checked his watch and stood. He towered over the principal in a black suit and shiny gelled-back hair, like patent leather. "I'll leave you to it, Jeff. Got another meeting."

"No, Paul. You stay," Dr. Arnold said. "This time I want her expelled!"

Dr. Marks looked at his watch again, then sat, crossing his legs, lacing fingers around one knee.

"So." Cartwright scratched his head. "Any witnesses, Xavier?"

"I don't need witnesses. She's done it before." He pointed a shaking finger. "*She* was the one who super-glued my pants to my chair. The one who switched the signs, then barricaded me in the women's lavatory."

The dean and principal both raised their eyebrows at her.

Kristi raised one shoulder. "So what if I did? That doesn't mean I booby-trapped his desk. Even I'm not *that* stupid."

The dean bent and whispered something to Cartwright. Arnold leaned in, too, then his face got redder. "I don't give a fig how much her father donates. The little demon tried to kill me!"

"I'm sorry, Xavier," Dr. Marks said. "Without any witnesses, we can't very well throw—"

"Check the security tapes!"

Marks sighed, then nodded to Cartwright, who turned to the monitor on his desk and punched some keys. The school's hallways showed on the screen. He pulled up the intermediate wing and backed the video up until the hallway was dark and clear of students. There came the janitor, pushing the mop. A few seconds later, a flash of gray crossed the hall and disappeared into the darkened sixth grade cove.

"There!" Arnold cried. "You see? That's her!"

Kristi held her breath as Cartwright zoomed in. Close up, the screen showed only a blurry gray mass.

Marks shook his head. "Could be anybody, Xavier."

"Keep looking!"

Cartwright backed up and tried to follow the mass through the hallway and other cameras, but the Grey Ghost only flashed across the screen, never showing a face. After five minutes, the principal shrugged. "Sorry, Xavier. There's not any real evidence."

Arnold's jaw dropped.

"Her father's a powerful lawyer, Xavier," the dean said. "He'd rip us to shreds if we expelled her without proof."

Kristi leaned back, laced her fingers behind her head, and smirked.

Arnold stomped and sputtered like a toddler who'd been told he couldn't have candy for dinner. "You always let her get away with it!"

Cartwright scratched his head again. "Tell you what. Put her in detention until we get it sorted out. I'll let you know if I find anything more incriminating. As for you, Miss Connors..."

Kristi tuned him out, could have recited the whole lecture that followed word for word. *George Washington Prep is an honorable school. You must respect your teachers. Your father would be very disappointed,* and so on.

Besides, she could tell from his tone he wasn't going to look further. Her father's name was on the new library, after all.

But the principal *had* given Dr. Arnold permission to throw her in detention indefinitely. That might be worse than getting kicked out. She'd already spent three days in that dank, basement room after locking Arnold in the women's restroom. Another week, later, for the Superglue Affair. Now Arnold could leave her down there to rot for the rest of the year. She could confess now. But the thought of telling her dad she'd been kicked out of school made her skin crawl. Her mom would probably stick up for her, remind him she hadn't wanted to go off to prep school in the first place. But that could drive her parents even further apart. She gritted her teeth and crossed her arms, giving Cartwright the expected, "Uh-huh. Right. Got it."

Arnold swore and stormed out, slamming the door so hard all the pictures on the office wall rattled.

"I trust you'll take care of this, then, Mr. Cartwright." The dean followed Arnold out.

Kristi stood and started toward the door, too.

"Not so fast, Ms. Connors."

"What?" she growled and dropped back onto the couch.

He pulled a chair over in front of her. "I was your father's calculus teacher, you know. He was one of the first African Americans to graduate from GW Prep."

"*So.*"

"So, that means something. He was here on scholarship. Many of the students—even some of the faculty—didn't think he belonged. But he worked his tail off and proved those doubters wrong. Your brother and sister were honor students here. Doesn't Carrie work in your father's firm? Isn't Derek in med school?"

She looked away. She hated when people rubbed in how great the rest of the family was. Like she was nothing. Besides, he didn't know about her *perfect* dad's girlfriend.

"You're on a slippery slope now, Kristi. I've seen the scores from your previous school. You're bright. But keep up this mischief, and you'll be out on your tail, regretting it for the rest of your life."

Not likely. She clenched her teeth.

Cartwright leaned back. "Tell me why you dislike Dr. Arnold so. He has quite a background. Taught at Princeton. Wrote books about physics *and* history. You could learn a lot from him."

She almost choked. "He doesn't *teach*. He just grumbles and gives us tons of stupid busywork."

"He provides the opportunity to work and learn independently. To question the material. It's called guided exploration."

"Ha! Guided *boredom*, you mean."

Cartwright smiled. "I'll admit he can be dry and gruff. And I doubt he's ever had a student quite like you. But you two *could* be good for each other."

She snorted and glanced up at the clock. "Oh my. Time for gym class. Can I *go* now?"

"You *may* go. And stay out of trouble."

She rolled her eyes, showing him what she thought of that idea, then stomped out.

TWO

Ty sat among the other statue-still students as Dr. Arnold worked at his desk, muttering and scribbling in a notebook. No one made a peep. Kristi had been the only one ever brave enough, or stupid enough, to poke the lion. But Arnold had come back without her, looking angrier than when he'd left, if that was possible.

Ty glanced down at his book. *The American Revolution.* He'd skimmed his homework in the library after piecing it back together. But the chapter hadn't made sense. In England, he'd learned about the American colonies and their eighteenth century rebellion, but it had been a lot different than this book said. His British teachers claimed the colonists had been uncultured, greedy land-grabbers and smugglers who didn't want to pay their fair share of taxes; that the southern landowners only wanted independence because they feared Parliament would outlaw slavery and bankrupt them.

But *this* book said the King and Parliament were at fault for the war, that the colonists had been treated unfairly. *Taxation without Representation* was printed at least twice on every page. It didn't say anything about smuggling or slaves.

So which was it—were the colonists greedy or was the king's tax scheme unfair?

He skimmed through again, came across a familiar name: Benedict Arnold. He'd learned about him in England, too. This book said Arnold was a traitor. Apparently both countries agreed on that. He'd been a Patriot, a general in the Continental Army, but had started selling secrets to the British and eventually switched sides. He'd actually led British forces in destroying whole American towns.

But his teachers in England had gone further. They blamed Arnold for the death of one of his co-conspirators, a popular army major named John André. They'd said that after the rebels won their independence, Arnold fled to England, where he eventually died, scorned and penniless.

Ty rubbed his eyes, looked up, and found Jeffrey staring at him. The bully winked and mashed a fist into one palm. Ty sighed, lowered his eyes. If only he was living back in those colonies right now, instead of at this stupid American school.

But which side would he have been on, Patriots or Loyalists? Neither, he decided, shaking his head. He'd have stayed out of it. He closed his eyes, trying to imagine living on a small farm on the frontier, raising horses, growing his own food.

His chest suddenly felt tight. When it was just the two of them in England, his mom would take him to one of her friend's farms every summer. They'd ridden horses through the woods and picnicked in grassy meadows. He'd fed the animals, sowed and harvested crops, even shoveled manure. But he'd never minded the work. Those had always been the best two weeks of each summer holiday. He would sneak away early each evening and read under a tree until there wasn't enough light, then he'd lay back and watch the stars. You couldn't see those in London, or here.

His eyes burned. He rubbed them with one forearm, then glanced up to make sure nobody'd noticed.

Back in the book was a drawing of angry colonists holding a royal tax collector down, dumping boiling tar and feathers on him. Ty shivered and glanced back up at Jeffrey. The bully would probably get a kick out of that. Idiot!

***

The bell rang and the students quickly shuffled out. Dr. Arnold never looked up, just kept scrawling mathematical formulas until the classroom was empty. When he reached the bottom of the page, he stopped, scowled and snapped the pencil in two.

"No. No! NO!" He crumpled the page and tossed it over one shoulder. It bounced off the whiteboard and landed next to six others. He grabbed another pencil and started again on a blank page.

Ms. Prichart poked her head around the doorframe. "Umm, Dr. Arnold?"

He flinched and broke the new pencil. "Busy!"

Her eyes widened and she stepped back, a hand on her chest. "I'm sorry to be a bother, but—I have the letter you've been waiting for." She held up an envelope.

He whirled to stare at her. "MIT?"

She nodded. He jerked his drawer open and pulled out a leather journal and some keys, then slid down the aisle and past her, snatching the envelope without breaking stride.

"You're welcome," she mumbled to his back.

He hurried down the hall, slammed through a door at the end, then galloped down a narrow stairwell. At the bottom, he unlocked a door marked Private, and entered the boiler room. On the other side was another door with three deadbolts and a sign that said KEEP OUT! He unlocked each bolt, then pushed into a small office with a single hanging light bulb. He dropped the journal on the desk and peered at the envelope in the dim light. The return address read *Massachusetts Institute of Technology*. His hands shook as he tore it open.

> *Dear Dr. Arnold,*
>
> *Your appeal of the decision on journal review is denied. The committee has unanimously agreed your findings are flawed. The theory of time travel has been much debated, true, but your propositions are not grounded in scientific fact. This decision is final, ending all current and future appeals. Please desist submitting your inane proposals to us.*
> *Sincerely,*

Thomas A. Washington, President, M.I.T. Review Board.

Arnold's face twisted. He crumpled the letter and roared at the ceiling.

***

The fields used for outdoor gym classes sat on a wide plateau overlooking the campus, ringed with leafy trees teeming with autumn golds, reds, and yellow. The late morning sun loomed, taking the bite out of the chilly air. Ty stood at the end of a long line of students in blue mesh shorts and oversized gray t-shirts with GWP printed on the chests. Mr. Wilson, the gym teacher, walked up the line grunting and marking roll on a clipboard. He was a tall, muscular man who, despite the temperature, always wore t-shirts that looked two sizes too small tucked into short-shorts that showed off his thick thighs.

Ty edged forward, spied Jeffrey's fat head three quarters of the way up the line. Still too close for comfort.

When Mr. Wilson reached the other end, he blew a shrill whistle and the students dispersed. Some of the boys formed teams on the soccer pitch. Others drifted to the basketball court. Most of the girls migrated to the large square of concrete where they pretended to exercise by batting tetherballs around a post or bouncing a 4-square ball occasionally.

Ty made a beeline toward the closest stand of trees and crunched through the fallen leaves. Once on the other side, he'd be out of sight. He sat on a gnarled root beneath an oak at the top of the hill overlooking the campus, leaned back, and pulled a well-worn paperback from the waistband of his shorts. He'd finished reading *Johnny Tremain* with a flashlight under the covers the night before. But he *had* to read it again, had to understand where Johnny had gotten his boldness. Just an orphaned teenager with a crippled hand, Johnny Tremain stood up to the British occupiers of Boston at the onset of the American revolt. Ty flipped to the last chapter, found the words that had been playing in his head all day. *A man can stand up.* He scoffed. Stand up for what? How, when the odds were so unfair?

A movement at the bottom of the hill caught his eye. A figure in red flashed through the trees, then zigzagged up the hill. As it got closer, he made out a dark face and braids. *Kristi.* After Dr. Arnold dragged her out, the kids had laughed, saying she'd be expelled. But, as usual, she must've talked her way out of it. No wonder Dr. Arnold had come back so angry.

He wondered how Arnold had known it was *her* prank. At first, Ty had been too shocked to confess he'd seen her in the school early that morning. Then, when Arnold returned without her, he'd been afraid to say anything for fear of being blamed, too. Besides, it wasn't his business.

But now she was headed right toward him. Too late to hide. He leaned into the trunk and held his breath, tried making himself smaller. She veered off, would have passed right by, but a sudden nose-tickle made him sneeze.

She flinched, stopped, then glanced back. "What're you doing out here?"

He didn't answer.

"Are the others on the field already?"

He nodded, hoping she'd move on. Instead, she took a deep breath and stepped closer. Her lips quivered, as if she was either trying to smile or fighting sudden gas pains. Either way—it looked scary. "Thanks for not snitching," she said finally.

He felt his face heat and shrugged one shoulder.

"How was Crazy Arnold when he got back?" she asked.

He grinned. "Stomped about like a prat. Kicked the bloody desk a few times." His smile widened. "Then called you a few choice names."

"Yeah?" Her eyes gleamed.

"But he doubled our homework. Said we have to write another essay for tomorrow."

"Oh." Her shoulders slumped a bit. "Sorry—I guess."

"I don't mind. Kinda nice seeing the wankers in class get all worked up."

She laughed. "Wankers—I like that. They still horrible to you?"

He looked down, said nothing.

After a couple seconds, she rubbed her hands. "Well—I'm gonna go play soccer. See you 'round."

He raised the book again, felt her still watching. Finally, he heard the leaves crackle under her feet as she dashed off.

***

Kristi ran onto the soccer field. The boys stopped and stared, mouths open. She slowed and strutted like a peacock. "Miss me?"

"Hardly," Jeffrey scoffed. "They didn't kick your butt out?"

She smirked. "'Course not. Lack of evidence. You should've seen Crazy Arnold blubber like a baby."

"Yeah? Well, thanks to you, now we hafta write a stupid essay."

"Oh, quit crying. Let's play."

Jeffrey crossed his arms. "Got even teams already."

She gritted her teeth. The jerk always tried to come up with an excuse to keep her off the field. He couldn't stand a *girl* showing him up. She scanned the other faces, looking for someone to stick up for her. But the others always did what he said. She'd have to find another player to even the numbers. But all the other boys were already playing something else. No way one of the girls would come—they might break a nail. Then she remembered. "I'll get Ty to even it out."

"Who, Froggy?" Jeffrey sneered. "Yeah, right."

She ignored him, took off toward the trees. Ty was right where she'd left him, nose still in a book. "Hey! English! Come play soccer."

His face screwed up as if she'd invited him to come wrestle a gator. "You must be mad."

"Come on." She pulled him up by one arm. "You can't just hide. Jeffrey's an idiot. Stand up, show him you're not scared. Maybe he'll leave you alone."

"Yeah, and maybe he'll pound me into a mince pie." But he let her drag him toward the field.

Jeffrey's eyes narrowed like a hungry lion as they approached. He kicked the ball at them. "Heads up, Froggy!"

Kristi flinched, but Ty jumped up and trapped the ball against the ground with his foot. Then he flipped it up with the toe of one shoe, juggled it twice on his thighs, bounced it off his head and launched it back.

Jeffrey ducked and covered his head. "Hey!"

Kristi stared in wonder. "Wow! Where'd you learn that?"

He shrugged. "Oh, I've had a go at football a few times."

"*A few*? That was *awesome*!"

Jeffrey stomped. "Quit gabbing, girls. You're with me, Connors. Go with them, Frog-boy." He jerked a thumb at the other team.

Kristi winked at Ty and went over to her side. Jeffrey pulled his team into a huddle. "If Froggy even touches the ball, knock him down. Step on his face."

"Don't be such a wanker, Jeffrey," Kristi said.

"Shut up, *Crusty*. This is a man's game. Don't like it, go play hopscotch."

She rolled her eyes. "Fine." *Idiot.* The huddle broke and she jogged past Ty. "Watch out," she whispered. "They're coming for you."

Ty looked incredulous. "You got me into this bleeding mess."

Jeffrey started with the ball. He ran right at Ty, lifting an elbow, snarling. Ty skipped sideways and bent his knees. When Jeffrey was almost on him, Ty bent under the flying elbow and jammed the ball into Jeffrey's big feet. Jeffrey squealed and sprawled face first onto the grass. Ty took the ball, juked two defenders, and buried it in the back of the net.

Jeffrey sat up and spat grass. "Play defense, *girls*!"

"Aww. Is he too much for you?" Kristi laughed. "Better go play hopscotch." She danced out of reach when he tried to shove her.

Ty ran circles around everyone the rest of the game. By the time Mr. Wilson blew the whistle and announced the two-minute warning, he'd scored four goals and knocked Jeffrey down two more times. Kristi, who normally hated losing, found herself rooting for the little Brit, especially enjoying Jeffrey's tantrums each time Ty scored.

But now she was lined up outside the goalie box for a penalty kick, a chance to save some face with a goal. Three defenders made a wall in front of her, Ty on the left. She stepped up and launched the ball with all her might. But, just as she made contact, Jeffrey shoved Ty right into the ball's path. It slammed into his stomach with a sickening *THWAP*. He dropped like a lead potato and rolled on the ground, clutching his middle.

"HEY!" When Kristi knelt next to him, his mouth gaped in a large fishy O. "He can't breathe, you jerk!"

"Ooooh!" Jeffrey brought his hands to each side of his face in mock concern. "Better give him mouth-to-mouth." The other boys laughed and formed a circle around them.

Ty arched his back and pulled in a deep wheeze that sounded like a haunted house moan. His next breath came easier. He lay back, eyes closed, chest shaking as it rose and fell.

She jumped up. "You're an idiot, Jeffrey!"

"Sorry, didn't know he was your *lover*." He puckered his lips and made kissing sounds.

She pushed his chest with both hands. "Shut up!"

"Hey!" He pushed back. "I ain't afraid to hit no girl."

She pushed again. "Go ahead. I'm not afraid to beat a baboon."

A new chorus of *ooohs* went through the ring of boys, interrupted by a sharp whistle. Mr. Wilson was jogging toward them.

"You got lucky, Crusty," Jeffrey sneered. "Tell your boyfriend not to mess with me."

The crowd dispersed and Ty pushed himself to hands and knees. Mr. Wilson crouched next to him. "What happened, Jordan?"

"It was Jeffrey," Kristi said. "He—"

"Just an accident." Ty grimaced and stood. "I got knocked down. The ball hit me. That's all."

"No! Tell him what—"

"I said it was a *bloody accident!*" He glared, eyes red-rimmed with unshed tears. "I'm fine."

"All right," Mr. Wilson said, frowning. "Go get changed for your next class."

"I'll help him back to the school." Kristi reached for his arm.

"*I'm fine!*" He pushed her away and stormed off toward the building.

She ran to catch up at the bottom of the hill. "I'm sorry, Ty."

"You didn't have to do that," he said, not breaking stride.

She made a face. "Jeffrey's a wanker."

He turned, started to smile, but stopped. "Now he and his mates'll have a real go at you, too."

"*Pftt.* They don't scare me. Bring it on."

He stopped at the door to the boys' locker room and finally looked at her. "Thanks," he mumbled, then disappeared inside.

When the door hissed shut, she looked around. Because of her trip to the principal's office, she hadn't had time to change into gym clothes. So now she skipped the girls' locker room and went into the school building through a side door. Math, next. At least she wouldn't have to deal with Crazy Arnold until history the next day. Then she remembered: *detention.* She'd have to miss basketball practice.

As she passed the office, Ms. Pritchart waved, then stuck her head out into the hall. "Kristi! Been looking for you, dear. Your father's on the phone."

Her heart dropped. "Uh—sorry. Late for class." She spun to walk away.

"No problem." The secretary grabbed her arm. "I'll give you a pass."

Kristi slumped and followed her across the office, into a small room. The phone rang as soon as she dropped onto the hard plastic seat.

"Uh—hello?"

"Kristine. It's Dad."

She gripped the phone. "Hey. What's up?"

"You tell me. I just spoke to the principal."

"Wow. He's *fast.*"

"Not funny! Are you trying to get kicked out? You know how much I spend just to keep you there?"

"Yeah, but I'd rather be home with Mom." Her throat tightened. "Then you can come back, too."

He sighed. "We've been over this, Kristine. Your mother and I—we need some time apart. School's the best place for you right now."

"Ha! You don't know what it's like here, Dad. The kids are stuck up. The teachers are monsters."

"You haven't been there two months yet. It's not—"

"They only let me stay because of you. My history teacher is a racist."

He went silent, then exhaled heavily. "Listen here, young lady." The low, deliberate voice, the one he used when trying not to yell. "That's a cop-out. You're not going to blow off the best private prep school in the country because you can't get along with one teacher or a bunch of other kids. Suck it up and work harder. Hear?"

She made a face at the phone. "Yes, sir."

"Stay out of trouble, understand?"

"Yes, sir."

He let out another long breath. His voice softened. "Make the best of things, Kristi. That's what we all have to do. It'll be okay. I love you."

She sighed. "Me, too."

She hung up and rubbed the headache in her temples. She was stuck.

THREE

Hours after her last class, while the other kids played on the fields or hung out in the dormitories, Kristi lay with her head on a scratched desktop in Arnold's detention dungeon, a long skinny cell of four dull gray block walls and no windows that smelled like a wet dog. Three pairs of florescent tubes shone pale light and produced a constant hum. It had been faint at first, but with no other sounds to cover it, the hum had grown into a buzzing whine that raked the inside of her skull like jagged fingernails.

She'd dozed off a few times, had dreams about swarming bees, and snapped awake to wonder how long she'd been out. *Time.* The greatest torture invented. Was it four o'clock or seven? The wall clock was dead as the fly under her desk, hands stuck forever on 1:23.

She groaned and rocked in her chair to make it creak, eager for any other sound to block out the whine. Two heavy wooden doors bookended the room and she stared at the one leading to Arnold's fabled lab. Its bluish-gray paint was scratched and dented, scuffed with black along the bottom—from, she guessed, sneakered feet trying to kick it down. What could be back there, mutant monkeys with two heads?

Arnold had brought her into the detention room by the other door. He didn't speak, didn't give her an extra assignment or even tell her what time she could leave. He'd only grunted, sounding more ape than teacher, pointed to the

21

graffiti-carved desk, and left by the lab door, pushing it open just far enough to squeeze through before slamming it.

Her stomach growled. "Come *on*," she grumbled to the water-stained ceiling tiles. She could sneak up to the main level, find a working clock and maybe a snack. But Arnold would pop a valve if he caught her. She resolved to smuggle in a watch the next day to at least time her torture. Food, too. But it could already *be* the next day for all she knew.

Suddenly the whine of the fluorescents sped up, amplified like the whir of an airplane propeller. The lights flickered, then surged brighter until—

POP—POP—POP

She covered her head as shards of glass rained around her. Three remaining tubes flickered for a few seconds, then went out, one by one. The whirring died and the room turned black and silent.

"Hello?"

After a minute, one of the lights flickered back on.

A muffled shout came through the lab door. "WAAAAHOOOO! I did it! I DID IT!" *His* voice. What was Crazy Arnold so happy about?

She sat up, folded her hands, and smiled. It would drive him nuts to burst in and see her looking cheerful and content.

He never came. After a couple minutes, she stood and pressed an ear to the lab door. Hearing nothing, she tried the knob. Locked. She dug a hairpin from her pocket, fitted it into the keyhole, and jiggled until the lock popped. She pressed her ear to the door again. When no sounds came through, she eased it open.

An acrid stink burned her nose, reminding her of the time her mom's hairdryer had overheated and caught fire, setting smoke detectors blaring through the house.

But there were no alarms blaring in the basement, just the sounds of feet padding on concrete deep in the room.

She wound her way through a maze of stacked, water-damaged cardboard boxes. A pale light flickered ahead. She stopped at the end of the path and hid under a small wooden table.

She'd always imagined Arnold's lab being bright white with shiny chrome tables and countertops covered with beakers and osmosis machines with gleaming blue and green liquids. Maybe even lightning conductors connected to a slab—for human experiments, like in an old Frankenstein movie.

Instead, the *lab* was a dim, dingy closet of unfinished beams cloaked in cobwebs. Four flimsy card tables held half a dozen laptops under a flat-screen TV that projected strange strings of numbers and math formulas. Dr. Arnold stood in front of this, haloed in the soft light, a cell phone clamped between ear and shoulder. He plugged a camera into the TV. The strings of numbers were replaced by a picture of a white, clapboard church, its cross and steeple reaching high into a clear blue sky.

"I'm telling you it worked!" Arnold yelled into the phone. "I'm sending video now." He hit a few keys. "The camera was gone for two minutes. It came back with eight hours of footage. That's St. Francis's church. It burned in 1778 when the British held Philadelphia. But there it is, intact. Those monkeys at MIT can kiss a goat's butt!"

He listened for a few seconds, then went rigid, gritting his teeth until those familiar purple veins throbbed along his temple. "What do you mean, *more evidence*? It's NOT a *freaking* computer trick." He stomped a foot. "Fine, I'll get your *evidence*." He drop-kicked the phone. "Imbecile!"

He picked up a silver, metallic rod, held it to the light. It was as long as two paper towel rolls, covered with buttons. He plugged it into a cord hanging from one of the computers and blue and red lights flashed along its length. He set it on the table and hit some keys. A thin line stretched across the TV screen. Numbers appeared: 0—100—200—300...all the way to 2000, like a timeline. A red dot blinked between 1700 and 1800. Then the line curved into a circle and started spinning.

Arnold held the rod up with both palms, as if making an offering to the gods. "Move over, Einstein," he cried. "This is *my* history!" He bent the rod into a ring. When the ends met, the tiny lights circled, slowly at first, picking up speed with every pass. Soon they looked like one continuous fiber optic light.

The overhead fluorescents surged. A laptop sparked, fizzled to black. Wind suddenly gusted from the center of the ring, throwing paper about as if a huge fan had been turned on. Lab coat flapping, Arnold braced his legs, arms trembling as he lowered the glowing ring to his head. What the heck—was he going to crown himself King of the Crazies? The wind suddenly switched directions, sucking Kristi toward him. Another laptop fizzled and smoked. The lights flashed, popped, went black.

The wind suddenly stopped. The room was silent. The acrid smell intensified, burned her eyes.

After a couple seconds, the lights came back on. Arnold was gone.

***

Ty sat back from the computer screen and rubbed his eyes. He'd been researching his essay for Dr. Arnold, on the illegal actions of the rebel leaders that led to the American Revolution, for three hours. He'd found websites that said famous patriots such as Patrick Henry, John Hancock, and Sam Adams were all using their merchant ships for smuggling. That dozens of tax collectors and British officials had had their homes burned by mobs of colonists. Another site said thousands of colonists had stolen lands in the Ohio River Valley that the British Parliament had promised to Native American tribes. Others were accused of bribery, blackmail, and extortion. There seemed no shortage of illegal actions on the part of these alleged rebels, who called themselves Patriots.

Yet he'd found plenty of outrages committed by the British, too. Royal laws were passed that said the colonists in Boston couldn't meet in groups larger than four, even at church. Businesses were shut down without cause, bankrupting thousands. Hundreds of men were jailed without trials. The Royal Army had burned dozens of churches and farms, killed many innocent colonists.

It all gave him a headache. He was no stranger to wars. England had been involved in many over the centuries, committed hundreds of atrocities that were often instigated by the kings and queens themselves. All war was an atrocity, so of course both the Patriots and British were guilty. But who caused *this* war? Who was right and who was wrong? It seemed to Ty, the Patriots had been right to protect their freedoms, *and* the Crown had been right to protect her interests.

He groaned. Maybe if he just looked at individuals. But the contradictions deepened.

As the threat of war grew, John Adams, an ardent Patriot, had defended the British soldiers accused of the Boston Massacre and got them acquitted. Thomas Jefferson had written the Declaration of Independence, stating, "...that all men are created equal..." and George Washington had led the Continental Army and become the first president of the new, *free* country. Yet both had owned slaves until their deaths.

Then he remembered Benedict Arnold. He'd fought for both sides. Maybe his story would shed some light.

He found a website that highlighted Arnold's career. Arnold had made a name for himself as a brave, devoted Patriot, had put his life on the line at Ticonderoga, Quebec, and Saratoga. But he'd switched sides for twenty thousand pounds and a command in the British Army. Ty whistled and shook his head. Talk about conflicted! Was it more than money that made such a man sell out his friends, his country?

A different website popped up: *Traitor's Bloodline*. Benedict Arnold's family tree. The branches were heavy with hundreds of Arnolds spawned from Benedict's two marriages. His children had served in the British military. His grandchildren had spread throughout the world, to India, South Africa, Nova Scotia, and some even back to the United States. The tree stretched all the way to present day. Ty chuckled, thinking about their own Dr. Arnold. Wouldn't it be funny if he were related to ol' Benny? As a lark, he scanned the names for *Xavier*.

After a few seconds, he gasped, rubbed his eyes, then scrolled up and down through the line of descendants. There it was, plain as day.

Dr. Xavier Arnold, former Professor of Physics, Princeton University.

Crazy Arnold was the great-great-great-great-great-great grandson of America's most infamous traitor.

***

Kristi held her breath, listening. Where was Arnold? After a few minutes, she crawled out from under the table. The lab was empty, the flat-screen dark. Smoke eddied from two laptops. She went through the lab, into a small office on the other side. A desk there was buried under a snowstorm of papers, a swivel chair jammed into one corner. The shelves held dozens of books. Novels by Jules Verne, H.G. Wells, and Isaac Asimov. Many nonfiction works about physics. The bottom two shelves were stuffed with history books, most about the Revolutionary War. The fattest, most worn-looking was *Benedict Arnold, Revolutionary Hero.*

She pulled that one from the shelf and thudded it onto the desktop. Half the pages were earmarked, covered with yellow highlighter and Post-its. She read through some of the highlights: *devoted husband, military genius, brave, misunderstood, victim of circumstance.* That last one was underlined twice and starred.

"What the heck—"

The lights flickered. Her eyes snapped back to the lab, where the TV and laptops flashed blue screens. A tornado-grade wind picked up again.

She dragged herself through the lab, using the desk and doorframe as handholds. As she slid back into her hiding spot, the lights went out. A pop and a flash came, like an old-fashioned camera bulb. The wind died. Then shuffling and heavy, labored breathing. The odors of sweat and filth gagged her.

When the lights flashed back on, a skeletal figure stood swaying in the middle of the room, panting, swimming in a torn, filthy shirt that hung to the knees above shoeless feet, dirty and bleeding. The face was sallow, eyes sunken. A patchy beard covered cheeks and chin. Its bald head was smudged with soot.

She stifled a gasp. *Dr. Arnold?*

The teacher looked around, eyes unfocused, jaw slack. Then he threw his head back and choked a laugh. He reached under the table and snatched up the cell phone.

"It worked! I'm back!" he yelled. "No, it wasn't ten *freaking* minutes! I was gone two whole *months*. I saw it all!" He danced a clumsy jig, leaving bloody footprints on the concrete. "Of course I can prove it. Just have to go back. I ran out of money and nearly starved. Was almost hanged!"

The man *was* nuts! She had to get out of there. She scooted backwards, bumped into a stack of boxes and sent them tumbling.

Arnold's head snapped in her direction. "I'll call you back." He dropped the phone. *"Who's there?"*

She scrambled to the detention room, made for the door leading to the main level. Just as she reached for the knob, Arnold burst in.

"What're you up to, girl?"

She spun, pressed her back against the door. "N—nothing. Can I go now? Uh—please? It's late."

"Oh yes. Detention." His eyes narrowed. "What were you doing in my lab? What did you see?"

She made her eyes wide and innocent. "I—uh—don't know what you're talking about."

He scratched his chin. A greasy smile stretched his lips. "Very well. You may go now, Ms. Connors. Until tomorrow."

She grabbed her backpack, dashed out the door and up the stairs.

***

When the girl was gone, Arnold lifted the cell phone to his ear again. "No worries. Now I know just where I'll get the money we need."

FOUR

A few faint stars speckled the black sky as Kristi ran down the steps of the school and crossed the lamp-lit quad, barely noticing the chilling wind.

Her mind raced around Arnold's disappearing act. Must've been a prank. Right. He was trying to get back at her for tormenting him. That had to be it.

But his face! How could he have faked that scruffy beard, or looked like he'd lost thirty pounds? It didn't make sense.

As she hurried along the walk past the library, a door flew open, catching her shoulder. She went down to the concrete on one elbow. "OWW!"

"Oh, sorry." Ty pushed the door closed and stepped over her, looking worried. "You all right?"

She flexed the arm and grimaced. A quarter-sized patch of skin was missing from the elbow. "Perfect!"

"Didn't see you." He leaned to offer her a hand. "I'm really sorry."

She let him help her up, then chuckled. "Well, I knocked you down this morning. Guess we're even."

He smiled and rubbed his stomach. "Didn't you cosh me with a football, too?"

"Oh, yeah, guess so. Hey, what time is it?"

"Little after eight, I think."

"Great! Crazy Arnold made me miss dinner."

He dug into his bag and tossed her a banana. "Nicked it from the café."

"Thanks. What're you doing out here?"

"Muggin' up for the history essay. Did you *just* get out of detention?"

She rolled her eyes. "I'd have been there all night, but Arnold caught me in his lab."

"You saw the lab? I hear he won't even let the janitors in there."

She puffed her chest. "Well, I was *there.*"

"What's it like?"

She shrugged. "Oh, just a dirty basement with a bunch of laptops and a flat screen." What else could she say? Tell him about Arnold disappearing and coming back as a street person? He'd think she was crazy. She was beginning to wonder herself. "He's, like, obsessed with the Revolutionary War. Especially Benedict Arnold."

Ty's brow furrowed. "How d'you know that?"

"Some weird books. One about Benedict being a hero. Crazy Arnold highlighted a bunch of words that made the guy sound like a good-guy."

Ty opened his mouth, as if to say something, but closed it again.

She narrowed her eyes. "What?"

He let out a long breath. "Benedict Arnold is his granddad."

"Who? *The* Benedict Arnold? The traitor guy? No way! Wouldn't he be like—two hundred years old?"

"Not his *actual* granddad. I mean his great-great-great-great-great-great granddad. I found a website that had a Xavier Arnold listed as a descendent. I thought it had to be a different Xavier, so I kept searching, found an article in Princeton's student tabloid, *The Daily Princetonian.* Dr. Arnold was a professor there."

"Yeah, the principal told me that. So?"

"Well, the article said some pretty dodgy things about him."

"Why am I not surprised?" She smiled wryly. "What'd it say?"

"That he started lecturing about history in his physics classes. Called George Washington a lucky buffoon, railed against the founding fathers. Then a student discovered he was related to Benedict Arnold."

"So it's true! What else did it say?"

"That he was trying to invent a time machine. Had a few students working on it, secretly. Then the bloke who'd outed his relation to Benedict disappeared. They never found him. Dr. Arnold told everybody the bloke had been depressed. The reporter seemed to think Arnold had something to do with his disappearance. After an investigation, Princeton fired him."

"I bet he did it. He—" She froze. "Wait. *That's* what he's doing!"

"Huh?"

"He *did* build a time machine!"

"Don't be daft, Kristi. It was just a silly article in a student tab—"

She grabbed his shoulders and shook. "No, no. I *saw* him. And this machine with weird lights. He said something about Einstein, about making history, then—poof—he disappeared. When he came back, he was different—like a hobo. Even had a shabby beard."

Ty snorted. "Time travel is not—"

"I *know* what I saw! He vanished, went back—in time. We have to tell someone."

He gave a lopsided smile. "*Help*! Our teacher is a bleeding time traveler. *Right.*"

She ignored him. "I'll tell my dad. He'll know what—" She stopped, shook her head. "He'll think I'm making it up."

Ty laughed. "*I* think you're making it up. You can't just—"

"I'll tell the principal. The dean. They'll have to fire him—like Princeton did."

"More likely throw you in the nut house."

"But they don't know about Benedict Arnold or that missing student. You can show them what you found. They'll have to fire him!"

Ty raised his palms and stepped back. "Hey—don't mix me up in your cracked scheme. You're gonna get us both kicked out."

"So what? You hate it here as much as I do."

"Yeah, but I don't get to go home to a rich family."

"Anywhere's gotta be better than here."

His face reddened. "Oh, the rich girl says it's not so bad, so it must be a bloody holiday." He heaved his backpack and stomped away.

"Ty, wait. I didn't mean—"

"Bugger off!" he yelled, walking faster.

***

At 7:30 the next morning, Ty slumped into his desk in Arnold's classroom, still fuming. What did Kristi know about anything? Crazy rich cow.

She was right about one thing, though. He *was* miserable. But what else could he do, go live with his jerk stepdad? Ha! Go back to England and live in an orphanage like Oliver Twist?

He raked a hand through his hair. Someday he'd have his farm, a place where he'd live alone and do whatever he wanted. Raise horses. Mum always said he was a natural on horseback.

He took out his essay and read it over. *Benedict Arnold, Villain without a Country.* After he'd read through pages and pages of contradictions about the rebels, Benedict Arnold's actions were the only ones he'd judged truly criminal. The protests of the rebels were illegal to the British, yet heroic to the patriots. The British responses were tyrannical to the patriots, yet deemed essential by the Crown. But there was no argument over Benedict; both sides named him a traitor. Dr. Arnold certainly wouldn't be happy about the topic, but Ty had a scheme. Instead of keeping the essay in his bag until the moment he turned it in, as he usually did to ensure *he* got the credit, he laid it out on his desk in plain view.

Other students started wandering in. At 7:50, Kristi tromped into the room and plopped next to him, though there were plenty of open seats. She scowled. "The principal won't even see me. Will you go back at lunch and—"

He grabbed his bag and essay and moved to the other side of the room. Her mouth dropped open and her forehead furrowed, but she didn't follow.

Then Jeffrey arrived with his posse. He glanced at Ty and he grinned. "Been lookin' for you, Frog-meister." They settled in the desks around Ty, like wolves circling a deer.

Jeffrey snatched up the essay. "Wow! Thanks, Froggy. Just what I was lookin' for."

"Hey!" Ty said, reaching for the paper. He had to put up a little fight so the bully wouldn't become suspicious.

Jeffrey slapped his hand. "Now, now, Frog-boy. Finders keepers."

Ty sat back and happily shut his mouth.

"This'll be my best work," Jeffrey sneered. "You even left room for my name. Thanks!" He scribbled *by Jeffrey Sampson* across the bottom of the page.

Of course I did. Ty held back the urge to smile. *Anything for you, big-buddy.*

Then Kristi appeared next to Jeffrey. "Move it, dog breath! That's my seat."

Jeffrey smirked. "Oh, right. Better let you two lovebirds be together." He stood and bowed. "Lady Frog."

She folded her arms. "Give his homework back."

"No!" Ty jumped up. They gaped at him as if he'd just gone streaking across a football pitch. He sank back, tried to look sheepish. "H—he can keep it."

Kristi balled her fists. "You can't just let him—"

"Kristi," Ty said through gritted teeth. "Let him have it and he'll leave me alone. It's all right."

"That's right, Frog-lover," Jeffrey said. "Your *boyfriend* knows what's best."

She shoved through Jeffrey and his crew and plopped down, fists still clenched. The bullies laughed and moved to the other side of the room.

"Why'd you let him keep your homework?"

Ty suppressed a grin. "You'll see."

At 8:09, Dr. Arnold sauntered in, whistling. His face was sallow, eyes sunken. He *did* look rather skinny. Dabs of toilet paper stuck to bloody nicks on his cheeks, like he'd shaved with rusty scissors. But he was beaming, as if he'd just won a door prize. "Turn in your essays." He walked up and down the aisles, snatching papers. Jeffrey handed over the Benedict Arnold one, then turned and blew Ty a kiss.

Arnold stopped at Kristi's desk. "Where's yours, Ms. Connors?"

"You kicked me out. I didn't even know about it."

"Excuses, excuses." He sounded bored. He looked at Ty. "And yours?"

Ty lowered his head. "I, uh—forgot."

"What a shame," Arnold said, tsking. "I thought a Brit would have pages and pages to write about the scoundrel rebels."

"Uh, no sir."

Kristi started to say something, but Ty kicked her leg.

Dr. Arnold moved to the front and wrote their new assignment on the board: fifty pages of textbook reading. Another essay: Show evidence of rebel luck at the Battle of New York. "You have fifty minutes."

The class groaned like one large, wounded animal. Arnold ignored them. He pulled his center drawer open slowly, tensing like a kid turning the handle of a jack-in-the-box. When it opened without blowing, he relaxed, then glared at Kristi. She shrugged and smiled sweetly at him. He gritted his teeth and furiously started marking up essays.

"Do you *have* to antagonize him?" Ty whispered.

She winked at him and opened her book.

Ty flipped his own open. The picture at the front of the chapter showed George Washington standing in the bow of a small fishing boat amid a soupy fog and British warships.

Ty started reading. In the summer of 1776, General Washington was to hold New York City against a superior British force. He split his troops between Long Island and Manhattan. Since he had no navy, the British had been able to surround and assault both islands with ease. Thousands in Washington's army on Long Island were captured on the first day. Washington and the remaining troops were pushed back onto Brooklyn Heights and trapped. The whole revolution could've ended right then, if British General Howe had pushed on to attack the remnants of Washington's forces. But for some reason he'd held back. That night, Washington sneaked his troops across the East River on fishing boats and flat bottoms, hidden from the British warships by a thick cover of fog. The army escaped to New Jersey, then Pennsylvania, where they were able to regroup and keep the revolution alive.

Ty closed his eyes and rubbed the bridge of his nose. He could almost hear his British teachers calling Washington a coward for running away under the cover of night and fog. But this account painted his military tactics as genius. So which was it? A fortunate series of events or a masterfully executed scheme?

He glanced at Kristi. She had an elbow on the book, chin propped on one hand, scowling at the ceiling.

"You're going to get into trouble," he whispered.

"I don't care," she shot back.

"Shut it!" Arnold said, not looking up. He flipped to a new essay and frowned. "*Sampson!*" His eyes narrowed to slits and the throbbing purple vein in his temple was back. Arnold jumped up and darted at Jeffrey, shoving Ty's essay in his face. "What's the meaning of this *drivel?*"

Jeffrey looked sick. His knees bounced under the desk so hard it rattled. "I—uh—I don't—"

Arnold tore the paper in half and threw the pieces in the stunned boy's face.

Kristi looked over at Ty with wide, astonished eyes.

Arnold stomped back up the aisle. "Close your books, idiot hooligans. I'm going to tell you about a real hero. A great man named Benedict Arnold."

Books slammed shut. The students sat up, looking relieved and expectant. Ty raised his eyebrows at Kristi.

"Don't let incompetent historians fool you," Arnold said, lifting his chin haughtily. "Benedict Arnold was a true genius. Made his name as a shrewd businessman, a highly respected one. When the war started, he volunteered service and money to the rebel cause. *He* was the hero of Ticonderoga and Saratoga. Almost died on the battlefield, but never got the credit he deserved. There should be streets and towns named after him! A whole state, even. But Washington and the congress lacked vision."

Kristi scowled, cleared her throat. "Last time I looked, Dr. *Arnold*, this school was named after George Washington."

Arnold glared. He marched down the aisle and thrust his face within inches of hers. "Washington was a *fool*," he growled. "Not half the man Arnold was."

"Oh, yeah?" She leaned forward until their noses almost touched. "But sir—wasn't Arnold a traitor?"

Ty shifted in his seat as the teacher stumbled back as if she'd slugged him in the gut. His face turned pink, then blotchy red. Kristi straightened, smirking, as if daring Arnold to hit her.

He might have, if Ty hadn't swallowed a lump, cleared his throat, and timidly said, "Uh, Dr. Arnold, where are Benedict Arnold's descendants today?"

Arnold's head snapped around and the flush drained from his face.

Ty took a deep breath. "Is it really true he's your, uh—your granddad?"

Arnold jerked and sputtered. "I will NOT be talked to like this. Both of you, get out!"

"It's not his fault," Kristi said. "He's British."

"GET OUT!"

Her jaw jutted. Ty grabbed her arm. "Come *on*, Kristi."

He pulled her into the hall, where she turned to him, beaming.

"What're you so chuffed about?"

"Don't you see? Now the principal *has* to meet with us. We can tell him all about Princeton."

He shook his head. "You really are barmy, aren't you?"

She grinned. "Only if *barmy* means a beautiful and athletic genius."

"Yes, Kristi. That's *exactly* what it means." He rolled his eyes, then followed the crazy girl down to the principal's office.

***

Kristi drummed her fingers on the short table in The Box, otherwise known as the in-school suspension room. Ty sat across from her, face pale, as if he would hurl at any minute.

The Box was cleaner than Arnold's dungeon, yet equally as boring with only the single table and two chairs. The walls were bare, cream-white with no clock. More time-torture.

Her stomach growled. "What time it is?" With the excitement of Arnold's disappearance the night before, she'd forgotten her plan to smuggle in a watch.

Ty shrugged.

"I wonder what Mr. Cartwright's gonna do to Dr. Arnold." The principal had been off campus, so his secretary had kept them in The Box all day. No restroom, no lunch. Just wait until her dad found out. She'd asked three times to call him.

"Oh, he'll be notified, sweetie," Ms. Prichart had assured her. *As if.*

Ty shook his head. "I wonder what he's going to do to *us.*"

"We didn't do anything wrong, Ty. Dr. Arnold's the crazy one."

Ty chuckled ruefully. "No, we didn't do anything *wrong.* You just blew up his desk and broke into his lab. I only wrote an essay making fun of his ancestor and disrespected him in front of a class full of students. Maybe Mr. Cartwright will throw us a going-away bash before tossing us out."

"At least we'd be away from Dr. Crazy."

Ty's face reddened. He glared, opened his mouth to say something, then shook his head and closed it.

"What's so bad about home, Ty? I would think that you more than anyone would want to get as far from this stupid school as possible."

He let out a long breath and looked up. His eyes were watery. "I don't have a home, all right. My mum's dead and my stupid step-dad doesn't want anything to do with me."

Kristi's chest tightened. "Oh, I'm sorry, Ty. I—I didn't know. What happened?"

He stood, faced the corner. "About a year ago, my mum married a fat tax lawyer who constantly smells like cigars and scotch. We came to live with him in Philadelphia. But he didn't want me, just my mum. Six months later, she got brain cancer and died. But not before she signed custody for me over to Reeking Rick. The first thing he did was ship me off to private school to get me out of his rat hair."

"What about your real dad?"

"Never met the guy. Mum never talked about him. I don't even know his name."

"I'm sorry, Ty."

He shrugged, sat back down, looking strangely looser, as if relieved for telling her his secret. "What about you? You get to go home to a rich family who loves you if you get kicked out, right?" His voice didn't sound accusatory as it had the on the walk outside the library. It sounded sad.

"Not quite," Kristi said. "My parents have lots of money, but things are far from perfect. My dad left my mom last year, just picked up and left. No explanation, no reason, just left. He won't even talk to her. I skipped school once last year, went to his office. I saw him with *her*, a pretty young intern with a nose ring who sounds like one of the girl chipmunks when she laughs. Then I knew why he left." Her eyes burned, so it was her turn to face the corner.

"I'm sorry, Kristi."

She shrugged. "What're you gonna do, right?"

A sharp rap came on the door. She jumped and wiped her eyes.

Dean Marks poked his head in. "It's time, Ms. Connors."

"Finally! Dr. Marks, you need to know Dr. Arnold's doing some crazy exper—" She froze. Arnold was standing right behind him.

"Time for detention, Connors." Arnold's eyes gleamed hungrily.

She moved behind the table. "You can't make me go with him."

Marks shrugged. "Sorry, Ms. Connors. You can take up your complaints with Mr. Cartwright when he returns tomorrow."

"What about me?" Ty asked quietly.

"You're staying with me, Mr. Jordan."

Ty's face turned green.

"It's not his fault, Dr. Marks. I told him to—"

"That's quite enough, young lady." Marks stepped aside and motioned for the door. "Off you go."

Kristi growled, knocked a chair over, then stomped out the door, keeping plenty of distance from Dr. Arnold.

***

Ty sat in one of the leather swivel chairs in the Mr. Cartwright's office. His stomach turned over on itself.

Marks faced him, leaning back, legs crossed. "What do you think of George Washington Prep, Ty?"

He shifted in his seat. "It's all right, I guess."

"You have a great opportunity here. A chance at a world-class education. Would you rather force us to throw you out on the street? Would your father be happy with that?"

Ty stiffened. "He's *not* my father!"

"But he is your legal guardian. That's what matters. Now, why are you harassing Dr. Arnold?"

"I'm not! It's just he's—he's—" How could he explain? *Dr. Arnold's away with the fairies. He's cracked. He's building a time machine in your basement.*

Marks eyed him. "He's what?"

Ty let out a long breath. "Not what he seems. Did you know he was fired from Princeton?"

"Yes, I'm aware."

"What about the missing student? They think maybe he did it."

"Did what?"

"You know. He was—always talking about time travel. Maybe he—"

The dean threw his head back and laughed. "You've got quite an imagination, young man."

"Maybe it *sounds* bonkers, but Kristi saw his time lab."

"The Connors girl has been filled with wild stories since she got here. You're dancing with a dangerous partner, my friend."

"She's not dangerous."

"Wrong. She just has protection." His voice dropped to a sympathetic murmur. "But you—who'll speak up for you?"

Ty's shoulders drooped. *Good question.*

"Don't get yourself expelled for her."

"What about the lab, then? Have you ever checked it out?"

"Research is part of Dr. Arnold's job. He's entitled to some privacy."

"But...if he even *thinks* he's building a time machine, don't you think the school should know about it?"

The dean checked his watch, sighed. "Would you feel better if we went and looked for ourselves? Then would you let these wild fantasies go?"

"Yes!"

Marks rose and buttoned his jacket. "Okay, then. Let's go."

He led the way down the stairs and through the basement. He ignored the KEEP OUT! sign, unlocked the door, and pushed it open. Mountains of loose-leaf paper covered the desk in a small office. Empty Snickers bar wrappers littered the floor. Ty glanced at the bookshelf, spotted the Benedict Arnold book Kristi had told him about. He reached for it, but Dr. Marks ushered him through the office and into a larger room with computers and a flat-screen TV. Kristi was seated facing a card table with two laptops on it. Dr. Arnold stood over her.

"Hello, Xavier," Dr. Marks said. "Everything all right?"

Arnold jumped, spun. "What the—what are you doing here, Paul?"

"This young man was concerned for his friend. But I'm more concerned about Chronological Intrusion. Is our little machine ready yet?" He chuckled, then his face changed, eyes glossing over like a hungry dog's. "I'd like to go back to the '50s, buy into a small burger restaurant, rename it McMarks."

Kristi turned her head and Ty saw the gag in her mouth. She jerked and wriggled, rocking the chair side to side. She was tied to it.

"Hey!" Ty yelled and stepped toward her. "What the—"

"Not so fast!" Marks clamped one hand on his shoulder and dug his fingers in until it hurt.

Dr. Arnold grinned. "Welcome, *Ty*. You're just in time for the big show."

FIVE

G et off me!" Ty kicked at the dean's shins, but those strong meaty hands held him easily at arm's length. Kristi now sat facing him, tears running into the blue bandana tied around her head. No defiance was left in her eyes, only terror.

Arnold swooped through the lab, humming, typing on each computer with great flourishes, as if playing an overture. Instead of the staple lab coat, he wore a blue vest with silver buttons over a loose white shirt, sleeves rolled to the elbows. Also a thick leather belt, soft moccasins, and brown, rough-looking suede pants tucked into long socks just below the knees.

"What's the plan, Xavier?" Marks asked.

"Our money's no good back there. Since we've no gold bars lying around—" He patted Kristi's head. "—she'll be my cash cow."

Marks nodded. "And the boy?"

"You brought him. He's your problem."

"He knows too much. You have to take him along."

Arnold pursed his lips, studied Ty for a moment. "I may be able to get a few pence for him at the harbor. Always a need for cabin boys."

"W-where're you taking us?" Ty croaked.

"Not *where*, m'boy. *When*."

A lump formed in Ty's throat. "You mean—back in time?"

"Bravo. Not as dumb as you look. To 1780, to be exact." He picked up a long, silver rod covered with tiny lights, stroked it as if it were a kitten. "You're looking at the greatest invention in the history of mankind. Imagine the power to dine with great Egyptian Pharaohs, to plunder coastal villages with Vikings, to influence the drafting of the Constitution, to—"

"To invest in Apple and Microsoft when the founders were just geeks hanging out in garages," Marks broke in.

"Indeed." Arnold's eyes gleamed. "The possibilities are endless. We can rewrite history, remake an America where the ignorant *peasants*," he pointed at Kristi, "don't interfere with the educated, the elite, with some false, overinflated sense of power."

Ty snorted. "Just because she's black doesn't mean—"

"Oh, don't be overdramatic," Arnold said, rolling his eyes. "It's not about skin color, it's about breeding. The witless Founding Fathers lied to generations of Americans, gave uncultured nobodies land, voting rights." He folded his hands, cocked his head to the side and said in a high-pitched, sing-song voice, "*You're all created equal*—Bleh!" He stuck out his tongue. "Well, m'boy, we're *not* all created equal. We need a ruling class to make decisions, enforce order, to ensure America remains a superpower for the next millennium."

Ty snorted again. "Let me guess. You're the *ruling* class and we're just the peasants."

Arnold smirked. "Who better?"

Ty groaned and dragged his hands down his face. "You're a couple of real nutters, aren't you?"

Arnold patted his own chest in mock indignation. "I prefer 'misunderstood genius'."

"But why 1780?"

"You traced my family history. Figure it out."

Ty remembered his essay and goose bumps ran up his arms. "Benedict Arnold."

"Bingo. Bad luck foiled my grandfather's noble plans, tainting my family name for more than two hundred years. But that's all going to change, very soon."

"Enough talk." Marks pushed Ty over next to Kristi. "Get on with it."

Arnold hit a few more keys on the closest laptop. Red and blue lights flashed along the length of the rod. Marks stepped back.

Ty glanced at the door. He could dash around the dean and run for help. But who would believe him? Besides, he couldn't leave Kristi alone with these nutbirds. He took one of Kristi's bound hands and squeezed.

Dr. Arnold bent the rod into a circle. A deafening wind engulfed them, like the thrust behind a jet engine, wobbling Ty's cheeks, forcing his eyes shut. He clenched Kristi's hand tighter. A second later he felt his body launch, as if from a slingshot, and zoom through ribbons of light that streaked like neon streamers. Then the motion turned circular and he spun inside a giant cone of white light, screaming his throat raw. But he heard nothing above the roar.

The world twirled like a flushing toilet until he hit the dark center of the universe and everything went black.

***

Hammers banged the inside of Kristi's skull. Waves of nausea rolled through her as if she'd just staggered off the world's fastest Tilt-a-Whirl. She opened her eyes and bright light stabbed in. The hammers sharpened to pickaxes. She turned her head and threw up. The headache slowly dulled. She tried to wipe her mouth with one hand, but her wrists were bound. Ankles too. She smelled earth, manure. She rolled onto elbows and knees, blinking until her vision cleared, found herself kneeling in reddish-brown dirt, surrounded by tall green stalks of...corn? The sky was deep blue, the sun baking her like a cookie.

"Hello?" The vibration of her voice brought the pickaxes back, plus a fresh wave of barfing. Someone nearby groaned, sounding just as miserable. "Who's there?" She fought her bindings. The rope around her legs loosened a bit and she wriggled out. But the one on her wrists was too tight. She stumbled through the corn, the rope end dragging like a snake.

A lump lay in a furrow ten feet away.

"Ty!"

He groaned again, holding his head with both hands. His eyes fluttered open. "What happened? Where are we?"

"I don't know."

"I feel like a train wreck." He tried to sit up, winced, and fell back again. "No. Make that two train wrecks on the bloody London underground."

"Same here. You remember anything?"

He shook his head. "Don't know. The last thing I remember was the lab—and—and—"

Realization dropped on her like a bag of bricks. "The time machine," she croaked, her throat suddenly dust-dry. "Oh my God! It can't have actually worked? Can it?"

Ty jumped up, staggered, and nearly fell. "We have to get out of here!"

"Out of where? You mean—" She hesitated. "Are we *really* back in time?"

"I don't know. Maybe. Come on." He grabbed the rope between her bound wrists and pulled her through the rustling stalks.

"Where are we goin—" The rope pulled taut and she fell back.

Dr. Arnold stood a few feet away, gripping the tail end. His face looked pale, almost greenish—but he was grinning. "Welcome to *my* history, kids."

Ty lunged at him. Arnold stepped aside and shoved him down into the dirt. Kristi pulled at the rope. "Run, Ty. Get help!"

Ty pushed himself up, looking back and forth between them.

Arnold hauled Kristi closer by the rope and wrapped an arm around her neck. "Stay where you are, boy."

When Ty's shoulders slumped, she knew then he wasn't going to leave her. A twinge of relief fluttered in her chest. She wouldn't be left alone, with *him*.

Ty's knuckles clenched white. "You'd best not hurt her, you nutter."

Arnold loosened his grip. "No, of course not. Not...directly." Kristi jerked away and ran to Ty. Arnold kept hold of the rope. "But if you cause any trouble, I'll turn your little friend in to the first slave-catcher I come across. Know what they do to runaway slaves?"

Kristi's jaw jutted. "I'm NOT a slave!"

"Wake up, girl. You're black, in colonial America. Got any papers to prove you're free?"

"But—but—" Her head spun like she'd returned to the Tilt-a-Whirl. She staggered against Ty, who steadied her.

Arnold laughed. "So, what'll it be, m'lad?"

Ty gritted his teeth. "Fine. We'll do it your bloody way. For now."

***

Kristi's red polo clung to her as stumbled along the dirt road, drenched with sweat, wrists on fire from the rough hemp rope. Arnold yanked each time she slowed, digging it further into her skin. Ty walked beside her, arm around her waist. They'd been marching for hours. Once, Arnold had allowed them a moment's rest at an almost-dry creek bed. Its water had been brown and tasted like dirt, but it was wet. Once upon a time, she'd refused to drink anything but bottled water. Now she was too thirsty to care.

A house appeared in the hazy distance. As they got closer, she saw it was more of a shack than a house, with faded gray clapboard walls and thatched roof. A large, bearded man was dragging a hoe through the dirt in a field in front of the house.

They turned up the drive and a small woman in a gray shift appeared in the door of the house. The farmer dropped his hoe and met them at the porch. He was as big as a tool shed. He took off his straw hat, revealing matted jet-black hair. His face was tanned, leathery, beard speckled with dust. His dirt stained white shirt had a gray ring of sweat that started around its collar and went all the way to his stomach.

"Good day, sir," Arnold said, bowing. "Would you be gracious enough to offer us a bit of water to wash down the road dust?"

Kristi lifted her bound hands. "Help us!" she cried. "He kidnapped us!"

Arnold yanked the rope and she fell to her knees. "Shut your mouth, girl!" He glared at Ty, who unclenched his fists and bent to help her up.

She looked up pleadingly, hoping the big man would hit Arnold, or grab him, or something. But he'd just stared, face impassive. Kristi glared. He could have broken Arnold in half with his bare hands, but he just stood there, as if Arnold had simply disciplined an unruly dog.

"I'm sorry, sir," Arnold said, bowing again. "But she's sun crazed. I'm afraid we've come upon some misfortune and would be greatly indebted to you for your hospitalities."

"Aye," the farmer grunted and disappeared into the shack with the woman. He returned a moment later with two small loaves of bread and two bulging brown skins that looked like bloated water balloons.

Kristi clenched her teeth. She'd rather die of thirst than take even a sip from this heartless man. She glowered as Ty took a long drag. But her raw throat ached. Almost involuntarily, she grabbed the skin, filled her mouth, then shoved it back into Ty's hands.

He studied the skin, then looked up quizzically at the man. "What's this made of, sir?"

"Bull's bladder," he said plainly.

Her stomach lurched, but didn't let go of its watery contents.

"We're much obliged, my good man," Arnold said, bowing a third time. The man nodded. They left him there and continued along the long, dusty road.

Kristi tore a piece off of a loaf of bread and gave the rest to Ty. He took a couple nibbles and tried to give it back.

"You eat it," she said.

"But you—"

She shoved it away. "*Eat* it, Ty!"

He hesitated, then took a bigger bite.

There were miles and miles of *nothing*, just farmland and forest between tiny shacks and log cabins. Along the road, two horse-drawn carts had passed. Each time she'd seen a dust plume ahead or behind them her spirits had risen with hope that someone would help them. But neither driver even glanced her way.

Now she saw another plume of dust ahead. A moment later, a cart drawn by a fat mule came into view. The driver was old with a weathered face, long gray beard, and tattered shirt and pants. Kristi stared at him piteously, eyes pleading for him to help them. His brown eyes met her gaze, but he said nothing. Just glanced away and kept moving, like the others. She could have screamed!

How can the guy just drive by and watch Arnold drag me? Don't they see—? Despite the heat, a chill ran up her spine. *Oh no. He does think I'm a slave! They all do.*

***

After what seemed like a hundred miles, they finally stopped beside a river. Kristi and Ty collapsed onto a patch of grass under a tree, the first shade all day. It was then she noticed Ty's face—blistered, deep red. Her own was speckled with sweat, hot, but only felt slightly sore. She'd once asked her dad if black people got sunburned. He'd laughed. *"Yes, baby, we can get sunburned, too. But God gave us beautiful dark skin to protect us."* Her chest ached. She could almost *hear* his voice. Would she ever see him again? Then she remembered his girlfriend, Maria with the ugly gapped-teeth. The ache sharpened.

"You all right?" Ty asked.

"Let's see, Ty. I'm in God-knows-where. Heck, God-knows-*when*. Tied to a lunatic who wants to give me to a slave catcher. I am most certainly not *all right!*"

He sighed. "Sorry, stupid question."

"Never mind." She rubbed her eyes and let out a long breath. "It's not your fault. Where are we?"

Ty pointed across the river. "I think that's Philadelphia."

"What?" She stared, mouth open. The riverbank was lined with thousands of trees. Clearings held small cottages with sharp, triangular slate roofs. Beyond were larger two and three story houses with arches and pillars, a few larger churches or meetinghouses. But no crisscrossing power lines, no skyscrapers. No mammoth bridges or interstates packed with honking cars. No hazy smog.

The road, the farmhouses, the horses and carts had been strange, yes. But looking at Philadelphia, *her* city—now so small, so primitive—brought needle pricks up the back of her neck. What was in store for them on the other side of that river?

***

Ty's tongue felt swollen in his sticky mouth, his legs rubbery, moving mechanically by some will that didn't seem to be his own. But he kept a grip on Kristi's arm, squeezing occasionally to show—to pretend—he wasn't terrified. Arnold led them down a narrow, stone-paved street that smelled like a port-a-potty left in a steaming locker room.

"Check out the zombies," Kristi whispered.

A haggard party of soldiers trundled up the other side of the street. But instead of staunch-looking fighting men, they more resembled walking skeletons with gaunt cheeks beneath scraggly beards. Their uniforms were filthy and torn; some blue, others gray, all mended with a medley of colored patches.

Two men at the back carried a third between them, his arms draped around their shoulders, head drooping like a rag doll's. One leg dragged. The other had been cut off at the knee. A red-stained bandage wrapped the stump.

"Bloody hell!" gasped Ty. "Colonial troops."

Arnold led them along the wooden sidewalk, elbowing through the throngs, ignoring the complaints of those they passed. Men in waistcoats and wool breeches glared at them. Women with frilly mob-caps and laced bodices turned up their noses in indignation. A few small boys with vests over pressed white shirts and shiny shoes hid behind their mothers and fathers.

As they passed, a shoeless boy with a dirt-streaked face stopped and openly stared at them with his mouth agape, showing brown, crooked teeth.

"Lookee 'ere," he taunted. "Carnival's come ta town."

Two other boys with soiled knee-breeches and dirty, untucked linen shirts, laughed and jeered with him.

Ty lowered his head, felt his face burn hotter. He eyed his own grimy khakis, sweat soaked polo. He looked as if he'd been dug from a trash heap.

Arnold continued his hectic pace, eventually knocking into a man with a long white beard, shoving him into a brick wall. The old man's face reddened and he turned with fists raised, mouth forming a complaint. But he froze when he looked at Arnold's face. His eyes widened and he shrank back, both hands up in surrender. Arnold rushed past without even glancing at him. The geezer gazed down at Kristi and Ty and blinked. After they'd passed, Ty glanced back over his shoulder. The old man was looking after them, wiping his eyes.

After three more blocks, they turned a corner into a cool breeze that smelled of dead fish. At the crest of a hill the wide river came into view, speckled with dozens of skipjacks, schooners and flat bottomed canoes either tied up or making their way toward the wharf on the closest bank. Hundreds of cawing gulls wheeled overhead while others alighted atop masts and pilings. Moored at the end of the wharf was a brig with two tall masts.

Arnold grabbed Ty's arm and squeezed. "Don't cause any trouble now, boy!"

Ty wrenched free and after one shove, grudgingly preceded Arnold down a dirt path. As they neared the wharf, the stink intensified; rotting shellfish, stale sweat, coffee beans, and spilled whiskey. Throngs of seamen moved up and down the wharf, unloading baskets and nets full of the day's shimmering, flopping catch. Half a dozen men holding machete-like knives, arms as big around as Ty's legs, lined a long wooden table, beheading fish after fish with rhythmic *clomps* in time with the sea shanty they sang with deep, coarse voices.

Our carpenter being frighten'd, to Paul Jones he came,
Our ship she leaks water and is likewise in flame,
Paul Jones he made answer, and to him replied,
If we can do no better, we'll sink alongside.

Still dragging Kristi behind, Arnold led them toward the end of the wharf and the tall brig. The hull was deep red, crusted with rock-gray barnacles at water level, lined with propped-open gun ports. Its sails were furled, leaving an intricate web of lines strung along the masts and bowsprit. Beneath that hung a painted, double life-sized carving of a naked mermaid with flowing hair, one hand covering voluptuous bosoms. Ty gaped.

Dozens of sailors, white and black, scurried about deck and wharf, pushing barrows, rolling kegs, carrying canvas sacks amid the shouted orders and curses of a man leaning on a cane. The mate was hunched, grizzled, with matted gray hair growing in knots to the middle of his back. A long beard hung beneath his snarl, tied at the end with black ribbon.

"On w'ya, ya lazy rats!" he barked, swinging his cane at the sailors as they passed.

One young man carrying sacks of flour as large as Kristi on each shoulder didn't get out of the way quick enough. The cane cracked his bare back. But instead of complaining, or tossing one of the sacks onto the cantankerous man's head, the younger man only flinched, then picked up the pace and stomped up the gangplank as if holding just a gallon of milk in each hand.

Arnold stopped before another man in a tri-cornered hat standing about with hands clasped behind his back. His eyes were squinted black slits, set in leathery brown skin. He wore silky white socks pulled up to the knees, brown velvet breeches, and a long, blue coat, looking hot and irritable in the heat. He eyed Arnold and frowned.

"Excuse me, Captain." Arnold bowed. "Have you need of a cabin boy? His mother, my dear own sister, died of the ague. His pa was killed at Saratoga. I've nothing left to feed the poor lad."

Ty opened his mouth to contradict him. Arnold yanked on Kristi's rope and he closed it. The captain looked Ty over and scowled. "Eh. Too small. Runty even for a cabin boy, 'e is."

"Eats less. And he's a hard worker."

"He's not my uncle!" Ty shouted. "He kidna—" Arnold backhanded him and he fell to the cobbles. Hot blood trickled from his split lip.

"Hey!" Kristi yelled, and Arnold yanked the rope. She lurched forward and fell beside Ty.

Ty gritted his teeth, readied himself to lunge at Arnold. But one look at Kristi and he held back. He couldn't give Arnold any excuse to hurt her. He wiped his mouth with the back of one hand and pushed himself up again, glaring.

"Excuse him, Captain," Arnold said, bowing again. "The lad was brought up proper, but he sometimes forgets his manners. You'll find a blow from time to time keeps him in line."

The captain frowned. "A few lashes'll dull any sharp tongue." He looked thoughtful. "Five pence, then."

Ty lowered his head. Out of the corner of his eye, he saw the first mate strike another sailor unfortunate enough to be within reach. The sailor fell to the wooden planks, where the old man preceded to thump him with the cane three more times about the head.

"Beg pardon, sir, but he's blood kin." Arnold pretended to wipe one eye. "Couldn't think of parting with the lad for less than twenty."

The captain snorted. "I can pay two able sailors for a week on that."

"I'll give twenty for him," called a voice from behind them. Ty spun to look. It was the old man Arnold had bowled over in town. But now he wore a straw hat pulled down low to cover his eyes. "Need hands on the farm. Could use the girl, too."

The captain grunted and walked away, up the gangplank.

"Thirty pounds for the both of them," Arnold said.

"Sorry, friend. I don't have a purse that fat. Perhaps we could come to some—"

"Thirty. Take it or leave it. I'll get twice that at auction."

The old man nodded, keeping the brim of the hat low. "Just the boy then."

"No!" Ty held tight to Kristi's arm. "He's cra—"

Arnold clamped a hand over his mouth, pinched his back hard.

"I've a fine home with plenty to eat," the old man said. "It'll be for the best, lad."

Ty bit Arnold's hand and elbowed his gut. He broke away, but this time the old farmer caught his arm.

"Let me go!" Ty twisted and fought, but the skinny old bloke was stronger than he looked. He pulled Ty close and whispered in his ear, "Have no fear. I'm a friend." His face was stern, but the eyes beneath the hat's brim were kind, pleading.

Ty looked at Kristi. Tears were streaming down her cheeks. Then at Arnold, whose scowl bored holes through him.

He let his arm go limp and stood obediently. The farmer dug tarnished-looking coins from his pocket. Arnold snatched them up and started pulling Kristi away. Ty grabbed for her hands. Hot tears rolled down his cheeks, too. "I'll find you."

She sobbed as her fingers slipped from his.

"Kristi! Kristi!"

Her lower lip quivered, but Arnold pulled her down the wharf, out of sight.

When they were gone, the old man laid a hand on Ty's shoulder. He knocked it away. "You don't know what you've just done!"

"God knows," the man said. He grabbed Ty's arm and tried pulling him in the direction Kristi and Arnold had gone. "Come on, lad."

"NO!" Ty held his ground. "I won't go with you, either."

"But we must make haste."

"For what?"

The old farmer smiled. "Why, to free your friend."

SIX

Kristi stumbled as Arnold pulled her along the walk, still pushing through the crowds impatiently. Upon glancing at Kristi, some of the people they passed turned their noses up; others drew back from her with apparent disgust. A few seemed to frown at Arnold with distaste, too. But no one stepped up to help, as if a battered young black girl being pulled at the end of a rope wasn't anything out of the ordinary.

They passed a pack of scruffy, barefooted boys in tattered shirts and trousers who laughed and pointed at her, then followed them down the block.

"Dressed like a boy, she is," one taunted. She stuck her tongue out at him. He laughed and threw a rock. It missed Kristi and hit Arnold between the shoulders.

Arnold spun, face red. "Get outta here, hooligans, or I'll give you a thrashing!" He picked up the rock and lobbed it back.

The boys scattered, cackling.

"I *hate* kids!" he grumbled.

"And you're a *teacher*."

"Not anymore." He yanked her into a narrow alley between two buildings. It opened on a large square with an empty wooden platform. A dozen or so men stood in small packs or leaned against the crude, outdoor stage, smoking pipes, gesturing, laughing heartily.

They crossed the square and stopped at an iron gate in a long oaken wall between two barns. A short, stocky man who looked like a small bull stood by a wooden desk there. He wore a dirty linen shirt and tan breeches with patched knees.

"I've a servant for the auction," Arnold said.

The bull looked her over, showed crooked, brown teeth with more than a few gaps. "Got plenty o' room." He grabbed her arm.

Kristi tried to wrench from his steely grip. He only squeezed tighter and hauled her toward the gate.

"You can't do this, Dr. Arnold. *Please!*"

Arnold ignored her, wrote something on a thick leather bound ledger on the desk.

The bull opened the gate, shoved her through. She fell on hands and knees, skinning her right palm, ripping her khakis.

"Enjoy yourself, m'dear," Arnold called.

The bull slammed the gate, making the iron shudder.

Kristi jumped onto it, pulled herself up to look over the top. "Please! I'm not a slave!"

The bull swung a club. She dropped to her rear as it *dong*-ed on the iron.

The pen—she couldn't think of anything else to call it—was rectangular, about the size of a small gymnasium, its ground rocky and dusty. The only opening in the walls was the gateway she'd just been thrown through. To her right sat a long, shallow trough with murky water. To her left a table littered with rags and jars of white, goopy stuff that looked like the paste she used to eat in kindergarten art class.

Soft hands clamped her shoulders from behind, as if to help her up. She knocked them off and scrambled to her feet. An old woman with a weathered face smiled at her. Tufts of gray hair stuck from around the dull blue kerchief tied on her head. A shapeless burlap dress was cinched at the waist with frayed rope. Her skinny arms looked wiry, all sculpted muscle.

The old woman clicked her tongue. "Don' act the fool, chil'. Scare off the rich ones that way."

Kristi gaped. "What're you talking about?" She scanned the other captives. Shirtless men were scattered throughout, dark skin glistening as if they'd just come out of the river. A pack of women wearing the same burlap shifts as the old woman sat or leaned in the shade along the back wall. Three children sat with them; two boys who looked to be her age and a little girl who couldn't have been more than five. Kristi's throat constricted. "I have to get out of here."

She turned to climb the gate again, but stopped when she met the sad, empty gaze of a young slave, fourteen or fifteen years old. His bare chest was broad and muscular, skin a light chocolate. He turned away. His back was crisscrossed with ash-pale scars starting at the base of his neck, disappearing into his breeches. She slumped against the wall and buried her face in her hands. "Oh no. No."

"S'all right," the old woman said, kneeling next to her, stroking her hair. "Mama'll take care of you."

Kristi pushed the hand away. "You're not my mom. I have a mother. And I'm *not* a slave. My dad's a rich lawyer. We have a big house and three cars and—"

"Hush, chil'," Mama said. "Don' talk too addled. It gon' be all right."

Kristi shook her head. "How? How's it going to be?"

The woman's gray eyes shone as she smiled. In them was compassion and strength, not the dread and hopelessness Kristi felt. "'Cause you in God's hands."

***

Kristi sat propped against the wall in the shade as Mama fixed her up. The old woman hummed softly as she took three long, spiny leaves from one pocket. She broke them and squeezed clear gel from their centers onto Kristi's raw wrists. "Aloe," she said, "learnt the herbs from my mama. She a gris-gris." It stung, but when Mama wrapped them with thick, wet cloths the hurt abated.

"Can't be goin' roun' dressed like no boy," the old woman said.

Kristi was too numb to be embarrassed as Mama drew her tattered polo off her, as if she was a small child. Mama replaced it with a scratchy burlap shift and tossed the dirty clothes and shoes under the table. Then she took handfuls of the white goop and rubbed it on Kristi's arms and legs until they were shiny as smooth chocolate. She dropped a dollop on her head and rubbed it into her hair and face. "Make you look healthy," she crooned, sitting next to her, rubbing more on her thigh.

The gate swung open and the bull-man entered. He began calling out names.

Mama squeezed Kristi's thigh, then stood. "I hafta go, chil'."

"Wait!" Kristi jumped up and grabbed her arm. "You can't leave me."

"Don' got no choice, girl." She squeezed her hands. "Be strong. Jus' do what dey say. Be *strong!*"

"But I—I can't—"

"Yes'm, you can. Pray with all your heart. God'll see ya through."

Kristi stumbled back, heart ripping from her chest as if her own mother was leaving her. She slid down the wall, hugged her knees and sobbed. After a few minutes, she heard distant shouting. She paid no attention until she was grabbed roughly and pulled to her feet. "I'm talking to you, hellcat," the bull sneered as he pushed her through the gate.

She tensed, almost snapped back at him, but heard Mama's voice in her head. *Be strong.* She bit back her words and swallowed them. The bull tried to drag her up a set of wooden stairs leading to the platform, but she pulled from his grip, marched up on her own.

At the top, a tall, sweaty man in a black robe and white curled wig stood at a podium. She was on a small stage, surrounded by white faces, some dirty and unshaven, others cleaner, pink cheeked, all topped by white wigs.

The auctioneer started spouting a rhythmic chant. "Got six 'n ten—fresh from the Isles—nine 'n ten, seven 'n twenty—healthy lass, ready to work on the morrow—five 'n thirty..."

Men called out and raised hands, but something like heat waves crossed Kristi's vision, shimmering, blurring the faces. She staggered. The auctioneer grabbed her arm and held her up.

"Got six 'n forty—eight 'n forty."

"Fifty pounds," called a man with a harsh, scratchy voice. She couldn't see his face, only blurry black blobs.

"Sold!" The auctioneer brought down his gavel with a sharp crack.

Be strong. Be strong.

She bent and threw up.

***

A screaming in Kristi's head drowned out all other sounds as she was carried off the stage and dropped on the ground. The cobbles were warm against her cheek.

"Up with ya," came a deep, scratchy voice. She didn't move. "I said *up with ya!*" He nudged her ribs with his boot as if he was getting ready to kick her.

Be strong! She felt herself stand, waver in the hot sun. The man was fat with a scraggly beard and a nose like a hog's, nostrils staring straight ahead. His shirt was dirty brown, breeches stained and patched, hair matted, greasy black. He spun her roughly, then cupped her face, pressed grime-caked thumbs into her cheeks. His teeth were varying shades of brown, his breath rotten, as if something had crawled into his mouth and died. He heaved her toward another man. "Hold her 'til Mr. Hartfield collects her in the mornin'. Git sharp, now. No whiskey!"

"No sir, not a drop." The other man was tall and spindly with dirty, straw colored hair. A scarecrow. His eyes were different colors, one green, the other gray and empty like a marble, fixed straight ahead even when the green one shuttled back and forth. Brown juice dribbled from his lips. He spat a stream at her feet and chortled stupidly, looking dumber than Jeffrey—if that was possible.

The scarecrow dragged her through a set of barn doors. He clamped iron over the wraps on her injured wrists. She pulled at the heavy chain connecting her to the wall; it only rattled, as if laughing at her. "Sleep tight." He laughed, too, then left.

Light filtered through slits in the walls, showed specks of dust hanging in the air. She smelled sweat, vomit, and worse. As her eyes adjusted, she looked around. Men and women lined all of the walls. Her legs went rubbery and she collapsed.

Another chain rattled above her. A light hand touched her forehead. "Thought I tol' you to behave, girl."

"Mama!" She tried to jump up and throw her arms over the old woman, but the chain pulled taut and jerked her back.

The kind old woman knelt beside her, touched one cheek. "S'all right girl. Mama's right here."

***

Ty watched from the shadows between a tavern and a barbershop as dozens of men gathered in front of the stage at Congo Square, faces lit by torches stuck around the perimeter. A few wore white wigs under tri-cornered hats and long, wool coats too warm for a summer night. Others had on simpler waistcoats and wool breeches like costumes he'd seen on stage in England. The rest were clad mainly in varying states of filth.

From his hiding spot across the street, Ty could see only part of the stage between the legs of passing horses and carts. The old man—Haines, he'd said his name was—had left him under strict orders to stay hidden no matter what. He'd promised to return, with Kristi.

Ty had no idea why the old man was helping him. He didn't have any choice except to trust him, though, so he waited. But what if Arnold saw him? What if Haines changed his mind? Ty's head swam with terrible scenarios. Minutes passed like hours. Finally, unable to wait any longer, he stepped out of the shadows and onto the street—right, in front of a passing carriage.

The horse reared and snorted. Ty felt the wind of a hoof that missed his head by inches.

"Watch where ye tread, nincompoop!" The driver yelled.

Ty jumped back and grabbed a lamppost, panting. He watched for an opening between carriages and spotted a bald man riding up the street. *Arnold!* Ty scrambled behind the lamppost. Arnold rode past atop a swaybacked, graying creature that looked like a skeleton with a loose mule-suit draped over it. He passed on without looking Ty's way. But where was Kristi?

Ty watched him go around the square. Arnold stopped in front of a fat man on the opposite side and awkwardly swung down. As they talked, Ty crept closer, keeping to the shadows.

"That's righ'. Holdin' her in there 'til mornin'," the fat man said, jerking his thumb at a barn behind him. "I got yer forty pounds." He held out a leather coin purse.

Arnold frowned. "What treachery is this? The bid was fifty."

"Five fer the auctioneer, five fer me." He grinned. "You gets the rest."

Arnold took the purse, grumbling. "Best watch that girl. She's touched in the head. Full of wild stories."

The fat man chuckled. "Do tell. I heard 'em all."

Arnold dropped the purse into a saddlebag and tried to climb up again. The mule stepped back, tossing its head. Arnold fell, threw his arms around the beast's neck. He swung in front of the mule, narrowly escaping the stomping hooves.

"Yer gonna need a step-stool, m'lady," the fat man jeered, doubling with laughter and slapping his thigh.

Arnold's face turned fire engine red. "Uncultured heathen," he mumbled and tried to pull the mule back to him by the reins. It braced all four feet and stayed rooted.

"'Haps a side saddle." The fat man laughed until fits of cough overtook him. Then he slapped the mule's haunches with his big hand. The beast lurched, dragged Arnold on up the street.

Ty looked back and forth between the barn where Kristi was imprisoned and Arnold's retreating back. A lanky man was leaning against the barn door, yawning. Where the devil had Haines gotten to?

The money! Arnold had put the purse in the saddlebag. Ty could steal that money and buy her back. Tell the fat man there'd been a mistake. He followed Arnold past dozens of buildings before the teacher stopped in front of an inn and tied his pitiful mount to a post. He dug in the saddlebag, swore at the mule, then went inside.

Keeping an eye on the door, Ty crossed and came up alongside the mule. "Easy, boy." He stroked the poor beast's neck, then felt inside the bag, finding a wrinkled shirt and half-loaf of hard bread. No purse. He dug farther and felt something with hard corners. Pulling it out, he examined it by the dim torchlight on the corner. A journal. He stuffed the book into his waistband, and was re-fastening the flap when a hand clamped his arm.

"I told you to wait!"

Ty jumped with a start, then saw Haines's white beard and now—angry eyes. The old man tugged him into a dark alley between the inn and a tavern.

"She's in the barn down the street," Ty said, pulling free.

Haines nodded. "I saw."

"He sold her—like a horse or something. How can he do that? She's—she's—"

"Be still and wait here. I shall—"

Ty stomped his foot. "No. I'm not waiting anymore."

Haines took his hat off and ran one hand through sweaty white hair. "Very well. But if there's trouble, you must flee the town. Else we'll meet the gallows for stealing a slave."

A cold fist of fear gripped Ty's throat. He'd forgotten that two hundred years before *his* time, many punishments were not just harsh, but fatal. He managed a nod.

"I shall lure the guard away. You go in and find the girl. Make haste."

They made their way down the street. Ty ducked into another alley as Haines approached the guard. The two men talked a bit, both laughed. Haines offered a bottle. The guard's eyes widened, he glanced about warily, then the two men disappeared around the far side of the barn.

Ty rushed to the door, unhooked the latch, and slipped inside. It was pitch black. He gagged at the stench of sweat and human waste. After his eyes adjusted he could make out dark outlines lying along the walls.

"Kristi?" he whispered. "Hey—Kristi?"

"Ty?"

He moved toward the voice. She was sitting against the wall, knees pulled to her chest. When she saw him, her eyes overflowed with tears even as she laughed. "I *knew* it! I knew you'd come for me."

He reached for her hand. "Come on. We're getting out of here!"

The smile faltered, then dropped from her face. She lifted iron shackles and shook the rusted chain. "I can't."

He grabbed the chain and pulled, but the bolt didn't budge from the wall. "No, no, no!"

"Let me," said an old woman beside Kristi. She took Kristi's wrists and dug cloth wrappings from underneath the shackles, leaving them hanging loosely. Then she ran her hands over Kristi's head and rubbed something greasy on Kristi's wrists and hands. She held one cloth up. "Bite down on this, girl." Kristi did, then closed her eyes. The woman pulled hard. Metal scraped skin as the shackles inched up her wrist. Kristi moaned, tears spilling from her clenched eyelids. After a couple of seconds, one wrist pulled free. She fell back, cradling it against her stomach, moaning.

"Just one more, baby." The woman took the other hand.

As she pulled again, the door banged open.

Ty dropped to the dirt and rolled against the wall. Kristi and the woman sat in front of him. The guard swung a torch, sending shadows dancing. He staggered sideways, then grunted as if satisfied and left.

The woman went back to work. When the other hand pulled free, Kristi threw her bleeding arms around the woman's neck. "Thank you, Mama!"

"Ain't done yet. Git yourself over there by the door."

Kristi shook her head. "You have to come with us."

Mama laughed. "Too ol' ta study on runnin' now. But you— you jus' a baby. Don' ought ta be locked up in here."

Ty tried to pull Kristi away, but she planted her feet.

"I can't leave you here," she cried.

Mama smiled and touched her cheek. "I's gon' be jus' fine. Been in slavery my whole life long. You git yourself hid in that corner. Don' worry none 'bout ol' Mama."

"Come *on*." Ty pulled again. Kristi finally relented and moved with him into the corner.

Mama stepped out as far as her chain would let her. "Now we gonna git these chil'ens outta here." Nobody moved. "Come on. Make you some noise."

Silence.

At last, a young man on the far side of the barn started a low humming. A few of the people around him picked up the tune. They started rattling chains. Soon, the whole barn filled with the song, the clack of metal links, the thump of bare palms beating the wall.

The skinny guard burst in. "Stop that damnable racket!" The young man who'd started the song stood, puffed out his chest. He threw his head back and sang louder. The guard rushed across and elbowed him in the stomach. "Shut it, I say!"

The slave gasped and staggered back. Kristi and Ty slid along the wall and darted through the still-open door. Ty scanned the street. Haines was gone. "Follow me." They ducked next to a wagon going down the street and moved alongside it.

"Escape!" yelled a voice behind them. A bell tolled. "Slave loose!"

Ty dragged her down a narrow alley that reeked of garbage. They zigzagged through more back ways, darted across broader cobbled streets. Soon, the paving ended. Dark houses sat further back on the narrow dirt lane. They crawled under fences, staying off the road.

As they neared a dark building three times the size of the houses they'd passed, Kristi let out a sharp shriek and went down with a thud.

"What happened?" Ty asked.

She rolled over, grimacing, rubbing her shin. "Don't know. Tripped on something."

He found a rectangular rock jutting from the ground. He rubbed his hand across the face, feeling an engraving. He strained his eyes and made out a line of them marking the earth every five feet.

"I think we're in a graveyard." He reached down and hauled her up.

"Great. As if things needed to get creepier."

They crossed to the big church, stepping carefully around gravestones, and huddled by the wooden wall. The windows were dark, the black steeple outlined against the night sky. Small black shapes darted in and out of it. Bats. He shuddered. *Definitely creepy!*

The air was calm and hot, filled with the chirping songs of crickets. The road curved around the church and disappeared into darkness. A hundred yards into that dark was a flickering orange glow. Looking closer, Ty made out men on horses, carrying torches. "They're looking for you. We have to go back."

A muffled thud of hooves on the road rose through the darkness, accompanied by the creak and grind of wooden wheels.

"Get down!" Ty hissed. They flattened on the grass. The wagon stopped in front of the church. Seconds dragged like hours as they held their breath, trying not to move. Ty strained his ears, thought he heard shuffling. Then a weight fell on him like a sack of flour. The air wheezed from his lungs. Kristi gave a muffled cry.

Hot breath found one ear. "Shhhh. It's me," Haines whispered. He clapped hands over both their mouths. "Get in the wagon."

Kristi ripped the hand away. "No way!"

"It's okay," Ty said. "He's a friend."

She looked back and forth. "Really?"

Ty nodded.

She stood frozen for a moment, face screwed up in confusion. She took a deep breath. "Okay."

Haines helped her into the back of the wagon, covered her with empty potato sacks, and set some baskets on top. "You ride up front," he told Ty, who climbed up. Haines followed, then snapped the reins. The horses drew on, toward the glowing torches. As they approached, four men fanned out, blocking the road.

"Hold up," the lead rider called. He was much younger than Haines with dark hair and beard. A scar starting below his left eye crossed that cheek, bisecting his lips, stopped at the jaw. "We're lookin' for a runaway."

Haines shook his head. "Haven't seen anything. Been an empty road, all the way from Port Richmond."

The other riders surrounded the wagon. Scar urged his horse closer, looking hard at both of them. "Why you out in the middle of the night, old man?"

Haines shrugged. "Better than traveling in the heat of the day, nay? My two girls know the way home with their eyes closed." He leaned forward and patted one horse's rump.

Scar narrowed his eyes. "You a Tory, then?"

"I don't get mixed up with political nonsense. My son—" his voice broke. He took a deep breath. "—he joined the volunteers in the summer of '76. Died at Valley Forge."

Scar's look softened. He nodded. "On your way, then. Godspeed." He reined his horse back and the others moved aside, too.

"May God bless your journeys, men." Haines flicked the reins. The horses leaned into the harness and they ambled off into the dark.

SEVEN

Kristi woke in a room no bigger than the closets in her parents' house. The gray, slat walls were decorated only with dozens of dark knots and a small, greenish window with rippled glass. A tarnished brass candlestick stood on a table next to the bed, holding a stubby, yellow candle with a blackened wick and a frozen waterfall of hardened wax drippings.

She pushed the scratchy quilt off and sat up, grimacing at her sore muscles as she stretched her arms overhead. She spotted Ty sleeping on a pallet under the window. She rolled out of bed and the pine floorboards creaked as she stepped to him and knelt at his feet.

"Ty." She shook his leg. "*Ty!*"

"Bugger off," he groaned without opening his eyes.

"Come on, wake up." When she shook him again, he kicked at her and turned onto his side. "Great," she huffed, and looked around. A gray clay basin sat at the foot of the bed. She picked it up and heard an inch or two of liquid slosh. A little water torture would do the trick.

"*T-yyy*," she sang in a sweet voice. "Time to wake up." He snored on. She grinned and upended the basin over him.

"What the—?" He shot up sputtering, eyes darting around the room in confusion. They fell on her and narrowed. "Are you *mad*?"

"I warned you." She laughed. "Now get up."

His eyes fell on the empty basin in her hands and widened. "*EWW*!" He lunged to wipe his face on the rough wool blanket.

"It's just a little water, you big baby!"

"No it *wasn't*! You see any bleeding toilets around here?"

"What're you—oh!" She dropped the basin and covered her mouth, suddenly smelling the unmistakable odor of urine. "Ugh—I'm sorry!"

"What's *wrong* with you?"

She pinched her nose against the smell, but also to hold in a laugh. Her body quaked with the effort.

He rolled his eyes and his expression softened. "I save your butt and you toss pee on me."

A lump in her throat stopped the laughter. "You're right. I'm sorry." She dropped to one knee, grabbed his hands, choking back a sob. "They were gonna—gonna—"

"I know." He squeezed her hands. "But we're safe now. I *won't* leave you again."

"But where are we?"

"The old man's farm. You know—the Haines bloke."

Her stomach tightened. "So, am I—," she swallowed, "—*his* slave now?"

"No, I don't think so. He helped you escape."

"But why?"

Ty shrugged. "Don't know. Do you remember seeing him when we first got to Philadelphia, when Arnold bowled him over? He stared at Arnold like he'd seen him before and didn't like him."

"Who cares about that? How are we gonna find Dr. Crazy and make him take us back?"

Ty reached under the pallet for the leather journal. "I nicked this from Arnold's mule in Philadelphia. It's got all kinds of maps and notes, mostly dealing with Benedict Arnold, dates when he'll be certain places. To find Dr. Arnold, we're going to have to find Benedict."

"Fine. So where's Benedict now?"

Ty shook his head. "I don't even know when *now* is. We have to get back to Philadelphia."

Kristi's heart jumped into her throat. "We can't go back! They're looking for me."

"I know, but—"

A soft knock on the door interrupted him. He shoved the journal under the pallet as the door swung open. A woman's round face poked in. She had sparkling blue eyes, chubby pink cheeks, and curly gray hair.

"Thought I heard moving about." The plump woman squeezed between the door and bed. She wore a cream-colored apron spattered with flour over a long, plain cotton shift with sleeves rolled up, revealing flour spotted arms and hands. "You slept through breakfast, but I'll be calling Mr. Haines for dinner soon."

Kristi and Ty exchanged a confused glance.

"I'm sorry, dears. I've forgotten my manners. I'm Mrs. Haines, the farmer's wife. I do apologize about the modest quarters—" Her face flushed. "But I couldn't bring myself to compel either of you to suffer the barn."

"Our deepest thanks, mum," Ty said, bowing. "We're indebted to your kind benevolence."

Kristi furrowed her brow. Why was he talking all old-fashioned like that? What the heck did he even just say?

But Mrs. Haines nodded, seeming not to find it odd. "What are you called?"

"Ty, mum. This is Kristi."

"Kristi." The woman's smile widened. "A fine name, reminiscent of our Savior. You two must be near starved."

"Thank you, mum," Ty said. "But we don't wish to burden—"

She waved a hand. "I won't hear a word of refusal. Guests in this home shall not want for sustenance." She withdrew into the hall and shut the door.

Kristi stared at him. "Where'd you learn to talk so fancy?"

"Books, I guess. Ever read one?"

"Sorry, Ty. *I* have a life—at least I used to." She grumbled, held her stomach. "I'm too hungry to think. Can we at least eat?"

Ty nodded. "All right, food first. Then we sneak back into Philadelphia before Arnold scarpers."

They left the room, followed a narrow stairwell down, and went through a short connecting hallway. When they stepped into the kitchen, a blast of hot air hit them, laden with the aromas of stewing beef and baking bread. Kristi's mouth watered. Dried herbs hung from low beams overhead. A long tabletop was lined with a dozen mounds of dough and flour-dusty baking tools.

Her stomach growled. "Wow, smells great."

Mrs. Haines gave a quick smile as she stirred a huge black pot hanging in the fireplace. She moved to the brick oven, pulled out a golden loaf with a long, flat paddle, like the ones used to take pies out of the ovens at the pizza shop near Kristi's house.

"Excuse the heat, dears," Mrs. Haines said, dabbing her forehead with a kerchief. "Thursday is baking day. We'll take our dinner outside, in the fresh air."

They stepped from the heat to a small porch and a cooling breeze that smelled of jasmine, roses, and cut grass. Three horses, two sorrel brown, the third white with black pinto spots, stomped in a dusty paddock next to the house, noses buried in a water trough. A huge, green barn with gates opened to the paddock stood on the far side.

Kristi gazed upon the vast fields surrounding the farmhouse. Tall drying corn stalks filled the largest, seeming to stretch to the horizon. To the left of that was a field of waist-high golden grasses topped with white seedpods. The farmer was fifty yards out in the nearest field, digging among green shoots in black soil, his back to them.

Mrs. Haines stepped onto the porch and beat a triangle hanging from the rafters with a wooden spoon. The farmer wiped his hands on his shirt, then carried a burlap bag into the barn.

"You may wash at the pump," the woman said, pointing to a black pump handle sticking from the ground in the yard.

Ty rushed to it, dropping to his knees as Kristi pumped. He stuck his head under the stream of brownish water, raking hands through his hair, washing away the stinking wake-up bath. When he stood, water glistened in his hair, ran down over his polo. "*Much* better."

"Now what?" she said. "What if they ask where we're from? We can't say we're time travelers—they'll think we're witches and burn us."

"Nah, probably hang us, not fry us."

"*Ty!*"

He laughed. "This is *your* country. Don't you know anything about its history? The witch trials were in New England, not Pennsylvania. Of course, you *are* a runaway slave now. Probably not very educated." He winked.

She punched his arm. "Not funny, Brit-wit. Like I said, I have a life. Don't keep my nose buried in boring books. Besides, aren't you Brits and your *Tory* friends trying to over-tax these guys and steal their homes? See, I do know *some* things."

He frowned. "Uh—yeah, something like that."

They crossed to a plank table set beneath a spreading, shady oak.

Mr. Haines came out of the barn, looking as if he'd just been dug up from the garden himself. His white beard was dusty, his suspendered pants crusted with dirt, and his sweat-soaked shirt clung to his thin frame. He took off his wide brimmed hat and knelt by the pump, dipping his head in the water and shaking it like a shaggy dog in a bath. When he stood, water streamed from his hair and beard. He looked at them, glanced toward the house, then crossed the yard. His forehead was wrinkled, as if concerned. He sat on the bench across from them, but didn't say anything.

Ty cleared his throat. "Uh, thank you, sir—for helping us."

"Thank me later." Haines's gaze darted toward the house again. Mrs. Haines had just then stepped from the porch and was approaching with a glazed pitcher and four mugs.

"Thank you, Mrs. Haines," he said as she filled his mug with the same brownish water Ty'd washed in. She waited while Haines drained it, then filled it again and went back into the house, returning a moment later with a tray loaded with a loaf of bread and four steaming bowls. She sat next to her husband and the couple folded their hands. Ty nudged Kristi, and they did the same.

"Dear Lord," Haines said, lowering his head. "Bless our weary, afflicted visitors with Your bounty, and us with the strength to do unto others as You would will it. Bless our sweet Joshua, that he now knows no pain, only Your wonders to behold for all eternity. Amen."

Mrs. Haines kept her head bowed a moment longer, lips moving soundlessly. When she looked up, her eyes glistened.

"Was Joshua your... son, Mr. Haines?" Ty asked. "The one you told the men about, back in Philadelphia?"

Haines nodded, blinking. Kristi couldn't tell if his eyes were wet from the pump or if those were fresh tears. "Joshua was at Valley Forge in '76. A physician, not a soldier. But dysentery doesn't care if one has been sent to kill, or to heal."

"This Godforsaken war!" Mrs. Haines' voice caught on a sob. Her husband squeezed her hand. She took a deep breath and wiped her eyes. "Forgive me, dears. Now—where are you from?"

Ty glanced at Kristi. "Well, we—"

"Don't you recall, Mrs. Haines?" the farmer interrupted. "The boy's uncle sent these young folk to me to help with the harvest."

Kristi choked on a mouthful of stew. *Uncle?* She'd thought Haines was helping them because he hadn't believed Arnold story. But, then why would he lie to his wife? Why didn't he tell her about sneaking her out of Philadelphia in the back of the wagon?

"Oh, yes, I-I do recall now." But the way her eyes shifted between them, Kristi could tell she wasn't convinced. "And you, my dear? Are you his uncle's servant?"

Kristi dropped her spoon. "Not in a *million* years!"

Mr. Haines stiffened. "You know how I feel about that evil institution, Martha. The girl is no more slave than you or I."

Ty shifted on the bench. "My *uncle* has—taken ill, I'm afraid, Mr. Haines. We must get back to Philadelphia and find him."

Haines shook his head. "The city is no place for either of you. Besides, your uncle will have left town already."

"What?" Kristi said. "But we have—" She stopped herself. How did *he* know what Arnold was going to do? What game was he playing? "I mean, we have to find him."

"Of course." The farmer's voice was even, unaffected, but the creases in his forehead deepened like trenches. One hand was balled into a fist beside his bowl, the other gripped his spoon so hard the knuckles stood out like white marbles. He took a bite of the stew, chewed slowly, as if buying time, then spoke again. "I shall be going to the market at the end of the month. I'll take the two of you along."

"We can't wait until the end of the month!" Kristi smacked the table. "We have to find him *now!*"

Mrs. Haines's eyes widened with surprise. "Such tones to your elders, girl."

Haines laid a hand on hers. "It's all right, Martha. These children have been through a terrible trial recently. It's no wonder they are out of sorts."

"Out of sorts?" Kristi balked. "We're not—OWW!"

Ty pinched her arm. "I'm sorry, Mr. and Mrs. Haines," he said. "We *are* out of sorts. But, please, you don't understand." He hesitated. "We're not—from here, but rather a long way off. My uncle—he's the only one who can get us back home again."

The creases in Haines's forehead sharpened. "Xavier Arnold doesn't give two figs about taking either of you home."

"Wait!" Kristi rose from the bench. "How do you know his name?"

Mrs. Haines frowned. "What nonsense is this girl speaking?"

Haines ran his hands through his hair. "Nothing to concern yourself with, my dear. The man is merely an acquaintance."

"You know him, don't you?" Ty said. "Dr. Arnold. I saw the way you looked at him in town."

"Know him?" He glanced at his wife, then back at Ty, letting out a long breath. "I was once his student."

"That's impossible," Kristi said. "He's not even—"

"From here?" Haines cut in. "No. *Nor am I.*" He took his wife's hands. "I'm sorry, Martha. I've tried so many times to confess it all to you, but—I could never discover a way to explain without sounding—addled."

She blinked, whispered, "Tell me what, Stephen?"

"That I'm not from this place—or from this—this time."

She drew her hands away, shifted on the bench. "You are making no earthly sense." She crossed her arms and frowned, as if angry. But mainly, Kristi thought she looked scared.

Ty banged the table with one fist. "You're that graduate student from Princeton, aren't you? The one who disappeared."

Haines's face was ashen, suddenly looking a hundred years old. He nodded, but kept his eyes on his wife. "At twenty-one, I was in graduate school, studying the relationship of time and space through black holes. One of the professors, Dr. Xavier Arnold, took an interest in me, became my mentor. He said I was bright, talked me into pushing my dissertation aside to study string theory and time travel with him. He promised we'd be famous. I was young, so—I felt flattered. The great Dr. Xavier Arnold, noticing me! The university wouldn't sanction our research yet, he'd said, so we had to work in secret. But, you see—that made the possibility of discovery even more thrilling.

"Now, if I was merely bright, Arnold was a genius. But very eccentric, full of conspiracies and addled ideas posited around George Washington and the Revolutionary War. It was unnerving, I admit. But then, many of history's greatest scientists and inventors were once considered mad—Galileo, Archimedes, Newton, even Einstein. If Arnold wasn't a little unusual, he wouldn't have been studying time travel in the first place."

"Oh, my dear!" Mrs. Haines's face was paper white. "You've tarried in the heat too long."

"I'm sorry, Martha, but no—I'm fine." He lifted her hand and kissed it. She pulled it back as if he'd bitten it.

His shoulders slumped, but he continued. "After two years, we made a breakthrough. Discovered a seemingly viable formula and process, then spent the next six months developing a prototype time machine. But, from those first exalting discoveries, Arnold's obsessions quickly grew into lunacy. He raged against Washington in the midst of science lectures, revered Benedict Arnold as a hero, a martyr. He told me the first thing he'd do with our prototype was go back to Colonial America and set history straight."

Haines shook his head sadly. "So I started exploring his background, discovered he was a direct descendent of Benedict Arnold. When I confronted him, he threatened to have me expelled from the university if I told anybody."

"But you never attended university," Mrs. Haines said. Tears rolled down her cheeks. "Oh, my dear—"

"Bear with me, my love." He squeezed her hand again. "It was then I realized the enormity of what we'd done. I didn't want to *change* history, just see it and—" he flushed. "Get rich and famous, I admit. But Arnold was losing control. So I went to the academic dean, confessed everything: the studies, the models, the whole thing. The dean took me to Arnold and threatened to oust both of us if we didn't show him what we'd created. Arnold brought out the prototype, gave a speech about our gift to mankind. 'Imagine going back to bomb Berlin before Hitler's rise to power. Or destroying al-Qaeda before the attacks on New York and Washington,' he'd said. I jumped in, then, threatened to destroy the prototype, delete the files, burn the research transcripts. Then—a terrible pain in my head. I blacked out. And came to in Philadelphia—in 1740."

Mrs. Haines rose from the bench, trembling. "You are not just addled, but mad, husband. We must call on Dr. Gill."

Haines lowered his head.

"That dean." Ty said. "What was his name?"

"It was...Marks. Paul Marks."

"Of course!" Ty jumped up, almost knocking Kristi and the bench over backward. "That's how Arnold got hired. Dr. Marks is now *our* head-master. When I went to him to rat out Arnold, he turned me over to him. Told him to send us back here."

"ENOUGH!" Mrs. Haines grabbed her husband's arm. "You have been consorting with demons, husband. Come into the house, away from the heat and this terrible heresy."

"But Martha—"

"Don't *but Martha* me, Stephen Haines." She hefted him up by one arm as one would an unruly child. "If you have any sense left at all, you will retire to the house immediately."

He sighed and let her lead him inside, glancing back apologetically at Kristi and Ty, mouthing, *Later.*

***

Kristi shook her head and sank her face into both hands. "Could this get any freakier?"

"I hope not." Ty stood and went to the paddock. The black mare ambled over to the fence and he stroked her velvety nose. She snorted and lipped his fingers. He rubbed behind her ears, trying hard to wrap his brain around what was happening. He almost chuckled. He was living in a Jules Verne novel, hunting Morlocks in the past instead of in the future.

After a while, Mr. Haines came back.

"How's Mrs. Haines?" Kristi asked.

"Mortified." He gave a wry smile. "She's lying down now, convinced *she's* sun-addled instead of me. She'll be all right, just needs some time to—adjust."

"What year is it, Mr. Haines?" Ty asked.

"Please, call me Stephen. It's August, 1780."

Kristi gasped. "You've been stuck here *forty* years?"

"Yes, about that long."

Ty's forehead wrinkled. "Then why are you still just farming? You're educated—a *scientist.* You could make 'discoveries' that aren't supposed to happen for another hundred years or more. Outshine Benjamin Franklin and Thomas Edison together. Be rich and famous like you wanted. Live in a big posh house. Not be just a *farmer.*"

"Oh, yes." Stephen smiled. "There are a great number of things I *could* have done, like going to Congress, counseling George Washington on defeating the British in the first year of the war. But see, that's where Arnold and I differ the most. He saw history as a tool, to manipulate to his own benefit. But I believe our past, good *and* bad, makes us who we are *supposed* to be."

"But why?" Kristi asked. "If you told them how to end the war, you'd save thousands of lives."

"I fought with that idea, especially when Joshua enlisted." He gazed down at the table, took a deep breath. "But history is not mine to control, to judge and decide. The long, treacherous war has been harrowing, but it will also teach thirteen colonies to set aside differences and work collectively for a common good. With a quick win, there would be no reason left to unite. We would end up with thirteen country-states with thirteen rulers—and endless civil wars."

"Yeah. Like it was in Europe," Ty said.

"Exactly. I believe the purpose of this hard-fought, hard-earned revolution is to unite America for all time."

Kristi shook her head. "But what about slavery? *You* know what it's going to be like for all the slaves. You could save some of them—" Her voice shook. "—like you saved me."

He scratched his beard, nodded. "After watching my own son march off to war, seeing the evils of slavery up close has been the hardest to endure. But let's say I intervened. What if I freed Harriet Tubman's great grandmother, or Frederick Douglass's?"

"Then they'd be free! How can that be a *bad* thing?"

"It would mean Harriet Tubman wouldn't be there to lead hundreds of slaves to Canada and freedom, to inspire thousands of others to run away. What about the speeches Douglass will give against the Slave Act? The thousands of whites and blacks he will touch, showing both the horrors of slavery and what a former slave can accomplish with fair treatment and an education. If they are not first slaves, who will inspire change, lead others when the time comes?"

Kristi bit her lip. Maybe that made a little sense—but it wasn't *fair*.

"Enough about changing history now," Stephen said. "You're right. We have to find Arnold and get you two back where you belong."

"Will you return, too?" Ty said. "I mean—you could."

Stephen laughed. "Once, I would have leaped for joy at the chance. But I've grown old here. This is my home now. I'll live out the rest of my days with my dear Martha—if she doesn't have me thrown in the asylum."

Ty took the journal from his waistband and slid it across the table. "Here. It's Dr. Arnold's. There are all kinds of maps and notes about Benedict Arnold."

"I knew he'd come for Benedict someday." His lip curled. "Xavier Arnold doesn't care about preventing the Holocaust or other tragedies. It's all about him. *His* gain. He just wants to clear his family name."

"Can the journal help us find him?" Kristi asked.

"I don't know, maybe." Stephen took the book and scanned through the pages. "He's got some detailed maps of Pennsylvania, New Jersey, and New York. That's a lot of ground to cover." He flipped through, read further. "The last few pages are filled with notes about John André, a British Captain."

"Who is he?" Kristi asked.

"I've heard of him," Ty said. "Wasn't he a spy?"

"Yes. Benedict planned to turn West Point over to the British. André was his contact."

"So why does Dr. Arnold have notes about him?" Kristi asked.

"I don't know," Stephen said. "Give me a minute to think." He rose and took the journal to the paddock, leaned on the railing and flipped through it.

Ty and Kristi exchanged shrugs.

Then Ty's eyes widened. "Wait a second. Let me see the journal again."

Stephen tossed him the book. Ty flipped through. "You said it was August, 1780, right?"

Stephen nodded.

"That's it!" Ty slammed the journal down on the table and pounded it with a finger. "John André is going to be captured with Benedict Arnold's plans in September, 1780, one month from now. Dr. Arnold drew a map of where it happens."

"So," Kristi said.

"*So*, when André's captured, everyone finds out Benedict's a traitor."

Stephen scratched his beard. "So suppose Xavier goes after André to prevent his capture."

"But why?" Kristi asked.

Steven hit the table. "If André isn't captured—"

"Then nobody'll know Benedict's a traitor!" Ty blurted.

"Exactly," Stephen said. "Benedict turns West Point over to the British and becomes a hero again, this time to the Crown. It makes sense. Xavier can't go directly to Benedict without looking plain crazy or, at best, like a spy. Benedict would probably have him hanged." He chuckled. "Wouldn't that be poetic justice?"

"Hey, fine by me," Kristi said.

"By intercepting André, Xavier would be able to manipulate from the outside. Shield himself." He took the journal and studied it. "André will be captured at a crossroad outside of Tarrytown, New York on September 23. That gives us six weeks to find him. As I said, I'll be carrying the harvest to the markets in New York. An innocent guise that should get us past any roadblocks, British or Patriot. If you'll stay and help with the reaping, I'll take you both along."

"So somehow we stop Arnold from getting to André," Ty said. "Then force him to take us back to our time."

Stephen nodded, looking grim. "Yes. That—or die trying."

EIGHT

Kristi stood at the door of the barn in the dim half-light just before dawn, watching as Stephen and Ty gathered tools and loaded the wagon. The scratchy burlap shift she'd been wearing since the slave pen had begun to smell worse than the basketball socks stuffed in the bottom of her locker at school. But Mrs. Haines's dresses were way too big for her and Stephen had said it would push the poor woman over the edge if Kristi were to wear breeches like a boy. "It just isn't done," he'd said.

Kristi put her hands on her hips. "I don't want to spend all day in the kitchen. I've never baked anything in my life. Why can't I just come help in the fields? Is that something *girls* can't do either?"

She glanced back at the house, saw Mrs. Haines walk past an open window in the kitchen. The woman hadn't muttered a word, had barely looked at her, since telling Stephen he'd been *consorting with demons*. Now Kristi had to spend the day in that cramped kitchen with her. *Awesome!*

Stephen handed a long wooden pole with a curved blade attached to the end to Ty. "This is a different time, Kristi. You're place is helping Mrs. Haines."

"So much for Women's Lib.," she said, rolling her eyes. "It isn't fair."

"Sorry, Kristi," Ty said.

He looked funny, his slender frame swimming in a linen shirt three sizes too big and brown breeches that stopped short of his ankles, kind of like capris, held up with a length of rope. His large straw hat looked like a sombrero from a tourist shop. He grinned, swinging the blade above the dirt floor, miming cutting stalks.

"Mrs. Haines could use your help, girl," Stephen said, dropping a shoulder bag over his neck.

"I *don't* think so. She acts like we're crazy freaks."

Stephen gave an apologetic smile. "Mrs. Haines is still in shock. Give her time. She'll warm up again."

"But if you let me help Ty with the corn, she could have all the time she needs!"

Stephen took his hat off and ran a hand through his hair. "It's more than that. We're isolated out here, but visitors aren't unheard of. If a neighbor were to call, I wouldn't want him to see a black girl working in my fields. It would raise too many questions."

"Oh. You mean—slave catchers?" A chill ran up her spine.

"You never know. It's safer to lie low for a while."

She frowned and scratched her thigh under the burlap.

"All right then," Stephen said, turning to Ty. "Know what you're about, lad?"

"Sure. Pick corn, then scythe down the stalks and tie 'em up. Simple enough."

"Yes, *simple*." The farmer smiled. "I'll bring you some water after a spell."

Kristi and Ty left the barn together and crossed the yard. She stopped at the porch.

"Have fun," Ty said.

"It'll be a rave."

Ty went on down the hill and jumped over the creek that separated the yard from the fields.

Sighing, Kristi clomped up the wooden steps and pulled the door open. A wave of heat made her take a step back. *Yeah, a rave in a sauna.* Sweat immediately trickled down her back. She scratched her leg again and stepped inside.

Mrs. Haines, forehead sheened with sweat, stood behind the long pine table, folding a ball of dough about the size of a football onto itself, punching it, then folding again. She glanced up as Kristi crossed the kitchen, then dropped her gaze and hit the dough harder.

Kristi leaned against the wall, waiting for instructions. Mrs. Haines set the beaten dough to one side on a floured board, covered it with a dishtowel. Then she took another lump from a larger clay bowl and slammed it on the table.

Kristi jumped. She cleared her throat. "Can I help with something—ma'am?"

Mrs. Haines frowned, as if considering whether an insane person might be trusted with bread dough. "I would thank you to fetch some water," she said stiffly. The words were polite, but her eyes said, *Anything to get you out of my kitchen, Loony Tunes.*

Kristi grabbed a wooden bucket and went back out, grateful for the respite from the heat—and the angry woman. As she filled it, she gazed across the yard at Ty, who was at the edge of the cornfield, moving slowly. *Lucky little limey.* She lugged the bucket up the steps and took a last deep breath of the cool outside air before stepping back into the bread baking furnace.

Mrs. Haines nodded as Kristi put the bucket on the table. "Thank you." The hostility was gone from her eyes now. She only looked tired. "You ought to know I don't believe a word of Mr. Haines's wild tale. He is clearly not well."

"Yes, ma'am," Kristi said. *Anything you say.* She knew this game well enough.

The woman nodded so hard her plump chin wobbled. "Well, then. As long as you are aware."

"Oh, yes, ma'am. I am."

They spent the rest of the morning dancing around the edges of politeness, moving slowly into another sort of relationship. Mrs. Haines actually chuckled as Kristi tried to fold a ball of dough. "Put your back into it, missy." But after the first three loaves were in the close stove, she put Kristi in charge of them.

"If you should open the door early, they'll fall and be ruined," she instructed. "And if you should leave them in too long, the bread will be hard as stones. The smell alone will tell you when they're ready."

Clear as mud. But Kristi nodded. Mrs. Haines left to do laundry in big wood-fired kettle behind the house. The kitchen was all Kristi's. She pinched a leaf of sage off the herbs nailed to the rafters, opened each cupboard, eyeing dishes, clean rags, jars with red and yellow fruits and vegetables inside. She stepped to the window, but couldn't see Ty anymore. He was probably lying around tanning, having a great ol' time while she sweated like a fat man in a half-marathon. She leaned her head against the wall. Even dealing with that wanker Jeffrey would be better than this drudgery.

She thought about Thanksgiving the previous year, the last time her whole family had been together. Like every other year, she'd left the cooking to Mom and her sister and spent the afternoon watching football with her dad and brother. During the meal, she'd tossed peas at Derek when their mother wasn't looking, then ducked when he'd returned fire. They'd laughed and joked, like a real, normal family. Her dad left three weeks later, moved into an apartment downtown. When she saw him with that young, pretty intern, saw him touch the small of her back, the same way he used to touch her mom, she'd gotten so angry. She'd wanted to rush up right then, yell, ask what he thought he was doing. But she'd lost her nerve. Over the following months, it hadn't come back. She'd never questioned her father before, never felt like she had cause to—until then. Now she wasn't sure she *wanted* to know the truth.

An acrid stink made her nose twitch. *The bread!* She spun. A thin column of black smoke streamed from the stove up to the ceiling. She lunged, yanked the door open. More smoke billowed. She stepped back, coughing, eyes tearing. Thrusting the paddle into the stove, she slid the first two hard loaves out and they clunked onto the table like scorched bricks. But she moved too quickly with the third. It slid down the paddle toward her face. She threw one hand up and caught it.

"*Oooouuuch!*" she screamed as the blackened loaf seared fingertips and palm. She dropped it to the floor and cradled her burned hand.

Mrs. Haines appeared at the door, eyes wide. "What in providence—"

"I'm sorry," Kristi, said, coughing.

Mrs. Haines ushered her out of the kitchen, took her to the pump, where she pulled the handle and held Kristi's wrist so the hand was under the flowing water.

The pain intensified for second, then dulled as the water ran over it. Each of her fingertips was red and a fat blister was already forming in the middle of her palm.

"I'm sorry," Kristi said again, wiping her eyes with the back of one hand. She looked up, expecting to catch the woman's wrath. But instead, Mrs. Haines's eyes were soft, her face twisted with concern.

"It's no great matter," she said, pulling Kristi to her soft bosom, hugging her. "It's all right, dearie. Don't fret."

When she removed the hand from the water, the burns throbbed.

"Better?" Mrs. Haines asked.

Kristi shrugged. "A little."

"Come, let's put something on them."

They went back inside the house. Most of the smoke had dissipated, but the kitchen smelled like charred bread. Mrs. Haines lifted one blackened loaf and let it fall again with a sharp clunk. "Goodness, you could build a fine, sturdy house of these."

"I'm sorry," Kristi said again.

But Mrs. Haines started laughing, so hard she had to wipe her eyes.

"What's so funny?"

"It's so dreadfully like the first loaf I baked with my own mother!"

Kristi laughed too, then shook her head. "Guess I shouldn't plan on a career doing wedding cakes."

***

Ty stood at the edge of the cornfield, hat in hand, allowing himself a moment's rest to survey his progress. His hands were blistered and sore. His arms hung like gummy worms. A fly landed on one cheek and he twisted his lips sideways to blow it off.

Twenty full baskets lined the field. His fingers had blistered within the first half-hour of corn picking, so he'd torn strips from his shirt to wrap them. Then he'd cleared the stalks, estimating each row to be longer than three football pitches end-to-end. At first, it'd taken him four whacks with the grim-reaper scythe to fell each stalk, but once he'd gotten used to the motion, he could take out three or four with one smooth swing.

Now his muscles felt dead. He unwrapped his palms, winced at the bloody blisters.

Yet, despite the exhaustion, his body begging to simply lie in the dirt and sleep for a week, pride swelled his chest. This was *his* corn now, harvested with *his* sweat and blood.

As he took a deep breath and reached for the scythe again, the sweet music of the porch triangle rang. *Suppertime.* He looked at the cut field again, nodded, then headed down to the little creek. He stripped off his sweaty shirt and splashed his chest, sending exhilarating icy pin-pricks down his trunk. Dipping his head, he drank from cupped hands until his stomach bloated. Then he sat back, smiling at the sloshing of his swollen belly.

After a few minutes, he rose, found Kristi at the table under the oak. Her burlap shift was gone. In its place was a blue cotton dress, so long the hem dragged the ground. She dropped what looked like a large black stone onto the table and grinned. "So, what d'ya think?"

He stared. "Of what?"

"My *bread*, genius."

That's bread? "Oh. It looks—grand."

"I burned the first two, but Mrs. Haines said we can actually eat this one—the inside, that is. She's not so bad, you know. Didn't even get mad at me for almost burning down the house. What'd you do all day?"

84

He shrugged. "Cut corn."

"Is that all? We baked, like, ten loaves of bread and three-dozen biscuits. I burned myself, like, a hundred times." She held up her hands, showing white bandages tied neatly around nearly every finger. "Tomorrow, she's gonna help me make a dress that fits. Then teach me how to make butter. This is pretty cool!"

"Lovely." When he plopped onto the bench, the invigoration he'd felt by the creek drained like water from a tub. He yawned and lay his head on the table.

"Hey." Kristi sat next to him. "Where do you think Dr. Arnold is now?"

"Couldn't tell ya." He closed his eyes.

"What if we can't find him?"

Ty yawned again. "Don't worry. He'll be at Tarrytown with John André in six weeks."

"But what if we're wrong? What if he changes his mind? What if we can't find him, can't make him take us back? What if we're stuck here?" She shook his shoulder. "Ty?"

The only answer was a light snore.

***

That night Kristi lay awake on the pallet, sweating, staring into the empty darkness. She missed air conditioning.

She listened enviously to Ty's even breaths. She'd given him the bed, since he looked beat and probably needed it more. Big mistake. The straw on the stupid pallet itched and prickled her back.

When she turned onto one side the hard slat dug into her shoulder, so she flipped to the other. She couldn't slow her mind down enough to sleep. What will her parents say when they find out she's missing? Will it make her dad come back to her mom? But what if she's stuck back in time, like Stephen? She'll never watch TV or play a video game again. Never own a cell phone, or get to drive a car. Never play for the World Cup or in the WNBA.

Ty snored louder.

She groaned and got up. The stairs creaked as she descended to the kitchen. It still held the faint char of burnt bread.

Stephen's voice carried through an open window from the front porch.

"You wouldn't recognize the wonders of the future, Martha. There'll be huge machines that harvest fields in a single afternoon. Others that travel three times as fast as a horse, on wheels, and never get tired. Some with metal wings even fly through the air, carrying people around the world in a matter of hours. House lights will brighten like the sun with the flip of a switch, turning night into day."

"You will go back, then, I suppose." Her voice was slow, sad, resigned. "Find that man who first sent you here, and return to that mechanical Eden."

"No—never! My life is here, with you. This is my home."

She sobbed. "But what if something terrible happens in New York? You could be arrested. Killed! No—you must not go. The lord has already taken our son. I couldn't bear to lose you as well. The children can stay with us. They need not go to the workhouse. We can raise them as our own."

He sighed. "You know that's not our decision to make, Martha."

Kristi's nose itched. She pinched it to catch a sneeze, then backed away from the door and stole back up the stairs. She lay back on the straw and curled into a ball, staring into the dark, imagining she was in her mother's arms.

***

She awoke to sun streaming through the bedroom window. Ty was already gone. From the window, she spotted him kneeling in the potato field.

Down in the kitchen, Mrs. Haines was chopping vegetables.

"Good morning," The woman said, smiling. "Mr. Haines and the boy already ate, but I saved you some hot porridge." She set a wooden bowl in front of Kristi.

"Thanks." *Oh, man.* It looked like the slop Oliver Twist supposedly ate. *Why in the world would he ever ask for more?* She took a bite. The bland mush rolled in her mouth like soggy Jell-O. "Um—got any sugar?"

"Sorry, dear. Used it all in the baking. Mr. Haines was to buy more at market, but it seems he brought home some wayward children instead."

"Like Jack and the Beanstalk." Kristi grinned. "If you plant us, maybe we'll find a giant's castle in the sky, and all be rich."

Mrs. Haines smiled, but her eyes teared. "How my Joshua loved that story." She sighed and wiped her hands on her apron.

Kristi bit her lip. She'd meant to make her laugh, not turn sad. "Have there been any battles here?"

"Troops came through and emptied our winter stores, British *and* Continental. We used to own all the fields you see around us, but Mr. Haines had to sell much of it to pay taxes. Now, most of the harvest doesn't even belong to us. God has seen us through thus far, but I fear without Joshua's help, the burden will be too much for Mr. Haines to bear on his own."

"Oh," Kristi said, frowning. "I thought Joshua was a doctor."

Mrs. Haines's eyes gleamed. "My son wanted to be *everything*: farmer, doctor, lawyer, professor. Got ideas with every book he read, every lecture he attended."

"How did he end up in the army, then?"

"At sixteen, he went to study at Pennsylvania Hospital's Medical School. He studied all winter, then came home for the spring planting and fall harvests. The war began in his second year. He and his classmates joined the army as assistants. Joshua was at Valley Forge that first winter. He wrote home twice a week. Soon his letters were saying there wasn't enough food or clothing. Men had to wrap their feet in rags or tramp barefoot through snow. They suffered frostbite sleeping in tents. Some died of sickness every day, more than in all the battles.

"Then, in early January, he wrote that he'd come down with a flux, but expected to recover. The rest of the month we heard not a word. On the first of February, Stephen rode west to the camp to look for him. An officer said Joshua had dysentery and was taken by mule wagon to a hospital in Philadelphia. But God called our son before he arrived."

"I'm—I'm sorry." Kristi swallowed, gazing at the tabletop, uncertain what else to say.

"This *damnable* war!" Mrs. Haines slapped the table and Kristi jumped. "The rich men in New England and London argue over taxes, but it's our children who march off to die." She wiped her eyes on her apron. "I'm sorry, dear. Such language. Forgive me. Tell me about your family."

Kristi's chest tightened. "My dad's a big-shot lawyer. My mom's an interior designer."

Martha's forehead wrinkled. "A what?"

Kristi smiled. "That means she decorates people's houses."

"I see." The woman still looked puzzled. "How many brothers and sisters have ye?"

"Two. My brother is in medical school, like Joshua. My sister's also a lawyer. She works for our father's firm. My dad jokes he has an office reserved for me, too. But there's *no way* I'm gonna be a lawyer. Read big boring books full of statutes and cases, work on files all the time — " Her throat tightened. At least she'd *thought* he was always working.

"He sounds like a good man. Quite prosperous."

Her eyes burned. "Yeah. Well, we argue a lot. Mom says that's 'cause we're both stubborn mules. At night we used to play one-on-one in the driveway—but that was before—"

Before her.

"—before he made me go to a stupid sleep-away school," she added quickly. "Now it seems like every time I talk to him, I'm in trouble for something."

"I'm sure it's been trying for him too, my dear. He must be frantic with worry for you now. When Joshua left, he took my heart with him." Her eyes glossed again. "Life's been hard for all of us."

"I hate that stupid school! I'm going to make him take me out—if I ever get home again."

Mrs. Haines came around the table to hug her. "Mr. Haines will get you home, never fear. He's a stubborn mule, too. Doesn't know when to stop or how to fail."

***

Ty wiped his forehead and drew his straw hat lower. He felt like a stick of dried jerky. He'd woken as stiff as a tin robot left in the rain. Instead of the cornfields, today Stephen sent him out to dig potatoes, so he'd spent the morning hunched, digging hundreds of spuds from the black, stony dirt.

He stood to stretch and something popped in his back. He twisted and his spine popped like popcorn. His hands felt like raw meat. His fingernails were caked with enough dirt to grow their own potatoes. His back ached from bending all morning.

Yet, he realized he was smiling. Here there were no bullies to harass him. No dull teachers droning on because they liked the sound of their own voices. No jerk of a stepdad.

He was free. No, better than that. Stephen needed him, appreciated his help. He topped off the last bushel basket, wiped muddy hands down his shirt, and returned to the barn.

Stephen was cursing a streak as Ty stepped through the door. The farmer's face dripped sweat as he tried to slip the bridal over one horse's head, but the barrel-chested sorrel kept stomping, snorting, tossing her head to evade it. Stephen threw it down and swore again. "Belle's a spoiled princess today. Won't work in this heat."

"Can I try?" Ty approached the mare, who rolled her eyes at him and snorted. "Shhhh, Belle," he whispered, stroking her golden coat. She tossed her head. When he caressed her silken nose she nipped at his hand. "Whoa, girl. I know it's hot, but we've got work to do." He stroked slowly down her neck, humming the soft tune his mom used to sing to him when he'd fallen and hurt himself. The mare's ears swiveled forward. Her neck muscles relaxed as he scratched behind her ears. She shivered, lowering her head and bumped against his chest. He quickly slipped the bit into her mouth, pulled the bridle up over her ears.

Stephen whistled. "I've been fighting with her for the better part of an hour."

"She just needed a little more love." He patted her neck. She nuzzled his arm, blowing warm breath through his shirtsleeve. "I'll hitch her up."

"I'm off to the field to collect corn," Stephen said. "Join me?"

"Sure," Ty said and climbed up onto the bench seat. They bumped along the rocky, rutted ground toward the cornfield and stopped at the line of bushel baskets he'd filled the day before. Ty surveyed his work, the long rows yet standing, and sighed. "Thought I'd gotten further."

"Nonsense." Stephen clapped his shoulder. "That's more than I could've cleared in one afternoon."

Ty smiled. "I tried."

As they loaded the wagon, Ty's mind sorted through the events of the last week. What would his teachers in England say if they could see him here, helping a colonial farmer, one without a political agenda, simply trying to survive in a war-torn country? Would they still insist the colonists were insufferable, self-serving prats?

He watched Stephen work. In his previous life, the man had learned about American history from books and teachers, too. But the scientist-turned-farmer had *lived* it for the past forty years. What did *he* think?

"Stephen," he said. "Can I ask you about the war?"

Stephen dropped a bushel into the cart and turned to him. "Of course."

"My teachers in England say the colonists were greedy ingrates who tossed away their loyalty to the crown for money. But the American history books say the king was a tyrant who only wanted *all* the money."

Stephen grinned. "Trying to pick sides, are you?"

"I guess." He shrugged. "I mean, I'm English. I'm supposed to agree with my own country, right?"

"Loyalty is nothing to be ashamed of, lad."

"I know, it's just—I can see where the colonists are coming from, too. They're fighting for their rights, their homes. Brits have done the same before, too."

"I see." Stephen shrugged one shoulder. "Well, both sides are right."

"Ha! That's a *big* help."

Stephen laughed. "Money's a big part of it. The crown helped finance the first British voyages to America, all the way back to Roanoke in the 1500s. When they found success in Jamestown, the crown took control from the founders and made all of Virginia a Royal Colony. It did the same in Massachusetts and the other colonies. Over the next two centuries, hundreds of thousands of Europeans poured into the colonies and millions of dollars came back to the crown.

"Then, in 1754, war with France came. The crown sent money, guns, and troops to protect her colonies. They defeated the French, pushed them out for good, but nearly bankrupted England. The king and Parliament enacted taxes to make up that debt. They thought the colonies should help pay for their own protection."

Ty nodded. "Sounds fair."

"Some disagreed, though. A radical group known as the Sons of Liberty argued Parliament couldn't tax without asking the payers first. That it went against their constitutional rights as Englishmen."

"Taxation without representation?"

"That's what they called it. The Sons organized protests and boycotts on all taxed goods. Merchants soon felt the squeeze and started putting pressure on Parliament. Parliament eventually relented, and ended most of the taxes. But they held onto one, a slight tax on tea, more of a tax of principle, to show they *did* have the power to tax their own colonies. That infuriated the Sons, so, one night, they dressed as Native Americans and dumped thousands of pounds of British tea into Boston Harbor."

"But I've never understood the famous Tea Party," Ty said. "The people in England had to pay taxes to the crown. Why shouldn't the colonies?"

"But the colonists *did* still pay, just not to a crown three thousand miles away. Each colony prospered in part because of certain freedoms allotted by the crown. They'd been allowed to elect local representatives, make laws, levy taxes according to needs. Over seven generations, these homegrown governments had become accepted, and worked. Both sides were making money. But most colonists still considered themselves English citizens and remained loyal to the crown."

Ty nodded. "They'd gotten used to ruling themselves, though."

"Right. But after the French and Indian War, the Crown, in its need for finances, attempted to supersede the colonies' power. The colonists balked, protested paying more taxes to a far-away island that most had never even seen.

"Then Thomas Paine wrote in *Common Sense* that it was against nature for a king to rule a great land. That America ought to be free and independent. This notion spread like wildfire. More people began to question loyalty to a distant king."

Ty nodded. "I've always wondered how a small island country could keep control of so many colonies all around the world, the way they did for so long."

"I see it as like raising children. England was the mother. The colonies—America, South Africa, India, Australia—were her children. When young, children accept a mother to protect, nurture, help them grow strong. But a growing child needs a parent less and less. Of course, the mother never really wants to let go. Likewise, the Crown is still holding on with everything it has."

Ty smiled at the image of a pimpled, teenaged America arguing with Mother England about a cell phone bill. "Never thought of it that way."

"Thirty years after the war, John Adams wrote that the seeds of revolution were sown with those first crops in Jamestown. I agree. You can't dangle freedoms in front of men for seven generations only to jerk them away and still expect loyalty."

A ringing split the air. Ty glanced back at the house. Kristi stood on the porch banging the triangle.

"Dinnertime." Stephen climbed into the cart. "Hop on."

Ty shook his head. "Nah. I'm going to walk."

"Suit yourself." He nodded and pulled away.

They tasted freedom, then couldn't go back. Ty tramped down to the creek to wash. The kings let the colonists basically rule themselves for so long. I mean, what did they think was going to happen?

He knelt and splashed his face, gasping at the icy feel of the water. He felt as if he understood the colonists a little better now. He'd only been on the farm for two days and yet, despite the backbreaking work, he felt free. Why would *he* want to go back? To tormenters, bullies, blowhards. And a stepdad who'd never wanted him, anyway.

***

"We *have* to make a plan," Kristi urged in a sharp whisper that night, shaking Arnold's journal in Ty's face. The dancing light of two candles on the nightstand bathed their room in an orange glow. "We haven't even talked about how we're going to get out of here."

Ty yawned, sat on the edge of the pallet. "Come on, Kristi. We've got six weeks to make a plan. I'm knackered and we've got to be up again with Stephen at sunrise. Know how early that is?"

"Pshh," she said, putting her hands on her hips. "You'll survive."

"Fine," Ty grumbled and lay back. "Read me the part about André's capture."

Kristi sat next to the candle and opened the journal. Arnold's scrawls were barely readable, but she found the entry. "Here's what it says:"

Meeting with John André:
> *After months of written correspondence and passing information through go-betweens, Arnold met with John André on the morning of 22 September, 1780. Arnold passed the layout of West Point and the plans for taking the fort, which André hid in his boot. While they met, the ship which was to take André back to New York came*

93

under fire and left him. On 23 September, Arnold provided André with a horse, civilian clothing, and a passport with the name John Anderson, an American officer. At a crossroads outside of Tarrytown, New York, three plain clothed militiamen accosted André. Despite the passport, André was unable to convince them he was an American officer. They placed him under arrest, searched him, and found Arnold's plans. By the time troops arrived in West Point to arrest Arnold, the general had boarded the British Sloop-of-War, Vulture, and escaped to New York. André was hanged as a spy on 2 October, 1780.

"Jeeze, Ty, they hanged André? Poor guy."

But, like the last time she'd tried planning with him, Ty's answer was a snore.

"Wanker," Kristi said, rolling her eyes. She kept reading. The details of the capture were laid out in the next entry. André claimed the militiamen weren't arresting him, but robbing him, when they found the plans in his boots. When word got back to West Point that a spy had been caught, Benedict ran.

Then the handwriting in the journal changed, got messier, as if Dr. Arnold had been excited while he wrote. He wrote that if André hadn't been captured, the plans would have made it to General Howe in New York. He posited that Howe would have attacked West Point immediately and captured George Washington there.

Kristi whistled. *What if George Washington is captured? What will happen to America?*

She shivered, blew out the candles, and lay back on the pallet.

NINE

Kristi stood on the porch with Miss Martha's arm over her shoulder as the sun peeked from behind the trees and hatchlings in the oak chirped for breakfast. Clouds stretched across the sky, wispy and pink as cotton candy. A thin mist lay over the fields like a soft blanket against the damp, chilly air.

Kristi sighed, took in the scene. She was going to miss sunrises on the farm.

Stephen and Ty were off in front of the barn, harnessing Belle and Foxe to the wagon. Bushels of corn, potatoes, and wheat packed the wagon's bed.

The old woman squeezed her to her side and smiled, but her eyes were red-rimmed.

Three days earlier, Stephen had announced they were ready to go to New York to find André and Arnold.

A strange sadness had surprised Kristi. She'd spent almost every waking moment of the previous four weeks with Miss Martha: washing clothes, baking, sewing, feeding chickens, all the while chatting like old friends. She'd told Martha about going for tea on Saturday mornings with her mother. About trips with her brother and sister to amusement parks. She'd even mentioned her dad's girlfriend, but only once. Martha had been appalled. "In what sort of world does a husband forsake his family for—for—oh dear." Then Kristi had cried and Martha hugged her, told her it would be all right.

She was going to miss the sweet old woman.

Stephen tied down the last bushel of corn and pulled on his straw hat. "We're set."

Martha pulled her in, squeezed until Kristi thought her head was going to pop off. "If anything should go amiss, you come back directly."

Kristi blinked. "I won't forget you. Not ever."

The woman wiped her eyes, then hugged Ty, kissed his forehead. They climbed onto the bench seat of the wagon.

Stephen embraced Martha. "Have no fear, wife. I shall return."

Martha sniffled. "Tread prudently, husband. See that no harm comes to you or your charge."

"I'll safeguard them as our own, my dear."

They hugged for another few seconds, whispering too quietly for Kristi to hear. Finally, Stephen climbed up and flicked the reins. Martha watched them bump down the drive, waving a handkerchief.

Kristi let out a long breath and looked over at Ty. He was frowning, gaze distant, knees bouncing as the wheels jounced over ruts.

He'd changed as much as she had during the time on the farm. Even more. He was happy there. He never wanted to talk about their plans to get home. He'd put her off each time she tried to get him to study the maps with her. During meals, he only spoke of planting and harvesting. When they were alone and she'd brought up Arnold and André, he'd change the subject to nursing a horse with a lame leg, germinating summer wheat seeds, or the difference between regular corn, feed corn, and popcorn.

There'd been nothing to do but let him be. Obviously he was torn.

"Goodbye," she whispered as the house disappeared in the cloud of dust. She leaned her head back on the hard seat and let the rhythmic bumping lull her to sleep.

***

Nearly twelve hours later, when the sun kissed the treetops again, Stephen pulled the wagon off the unpaved lane and into a clearing in the trees on the banks of the river. "We'll camp here tonight."

"Finally!" Kristi said. "My butt hurts!" She jumped down and stretched.

Stephen stood slowly, carefully, pressing his lower back. He stepped down, wincing, braced one hand on the side of the wagon.

"You okay?" Ty asked.

"Just a little tight. I'd sell the farm right now for a bottle of aspirin."

"Lie down," Ty said. "We'll get a fire going."

Stephen shook his head, but when he tried to straighten, his face distorted with pain. Kristi spread out a blanket and he lay, grumbling. "Unhitch the horses. Give them some parched corn. Then gather firewood and go down for water."

Ty tended to the Foxe and Belle, then took a bucket to the river.

Kristi stepped into the trees—and a whole swarm of mosquitoes. She shrieked, danced and swatted. The insects whined in her ears, feasting. She gathered an armful of twigs and fallen branches, hurried back to the camp and dropped them, then pulled a scratchy blanket over her head. "Ugh! I *hate* mosquitoes!"

When Ty returned with a full bucket, they cleared a circle in the dirt and piled the smallest twigs in the center. Then they sat back, swatting mosquitoes and scratching.

"Got a lighter?" he asked.

"Sorry, must've left my blowtorch at the farm. Don't we just rub two sticks together?"

"There's flint and steel in the wagon," Stephen said. "Find a birch tree with smooth, white bark. Tear strips to stuff under those twigs."

Ty went for the flint and she returned to the trees, discovering an even larger swarm of bloodsuckers. "*Vampires!*" she cried, slapping her neck. She finally found a birch, its trunk like a long, white telephone pole. The bark pulled off in sheets, like thick homemade paper. She pulled five strips and ran all the way back to camp. Ty was kneeling next to the kindling with a black rock and steel rod.

"Wad the bark like balls of paper," Stephen instructed. "Pile it up, then strike the flint near the base. Once you've got a proper flame, put more sticks on. But nothing too heavy until you've got a good fire going."

Ty shrugged. "Sounds easy enough."

Kristi stuffed birch wads under the twigs. Ty leaned over the pile and smacked the steel against the rock. A quick flash of sparks rained on the pile. A few caught the edges of the wads, glowed for an instant, then shriveled out. He tried again and again, but couldn't get the sparks to glow for longer than a second, much less catch fire.

"Needs a woman's touch." She took the fire starters, spread her arms wide, then crashed them like cymbals. "*Owww!*" She dropped the flint and popped an injured thumb in her mouth.

"That's some woman's touch," Ty laughed. "You all right?"

"Fine!" she grumbled, grabbing the flint again. Keeping her fingers curled back, she slammed the fire-starters again. But the sparks died even before they landed. "This is stupid."

"Don't *smack* them," Stephen said. "Scrape the steel against the flint like a match on the side of a matchbox."

When she tried the move, a torrent of sparks showered onto the pile. She grinned, did it three more times in quick succession, making a golden waterfall. The edge of one wad glowed and a hair-thin tendril of smoke rose. Ty knelt and blew gently on its base. A tiny flame ignited, spread through the wadded birch strips. He kept blowing. After a minute, white smoke billowed from the center and tongues of flames licked up. Kristi laid bigger twigs on top. Soon she was dropping sticks as fat as her fingers, then branches nearly big as her arms.

After a few minutes, the fire roared, popping and dancing into the purpling sky. They stepped back to avoid singeing their eyebrows. She realized with relief that the mosquitoes were gone. "You hungry?"

"Starved. How about you, Stephen?"

No answer. The farmer was snoring.

They laughed. When Kristi stepped away from the fire, the bloodsucking horde dive-bombed her head again. She snatched the basket of food from the wagon and ran back to the fireside, where the mosquitos dispersed. She tossed a hunk of bread in Ty's lap. "So, where are we?"

He flipped through Arnold's journal, found a map of the Pennsylvania/New Jersey boarder.

"We crossed the Delaware River here, at Trenton." He drew his finger along the river. "We're here, about ten miles north of there."

"I wonder where Arnold is now."

He closed the journal and snapped a twig.

"You still want to find him, don't you?"

His forehead wrinkled and he didn't answer.

"Ty?"

"Yeah, only..." He threw the twig into the fire. "I didn't think I'd like it back here so much."

"But we don't belong."

"I know. It's just—I feel good here with Stephen and Miss Martha, useful. It's bloody nice to not have to duck bullies all the time." He sighed.

She nudged him, changed the subject. "So—Trenton, huh? Any cool battles coming up?"

The frown fell from his face. "Not now, but a big one happened at the beginning of the war. Ever hear about George Washington crossing the Delaware?"

"Duh, Ty. I'm not a complete idiot. There's a picture in our history book of him standing in, like, some dinky rowboat."

"Well, that probably happened right around here. The first winter, things weren't exactly smashing for the Patriots. Washington had lost almost every battle. His army didn't have enough food or clothes. Congress was about to take command from him."

"Whoa. They'd do that?"

"Other generals thought they could do better. Benedict Arnold was one. So, on Christmas night, Washington took his army across the Delaware in the middle of an ice storm. Many of his men didn't even have boots, yet they marched ten miles to Trenton, leaving a trail of bloody footprints."

She shuddered, imagining bare feet slipping, freezing in snow, sliced by sharp ice.

"They surrounded the fort and opened up, waking the Hessians camped there with cannon fire. They took it after a short battle. The only two Continentals who died in the battle weren't even shot. They froze to death. It was Washington's first big win, so Congress stayed with him."

"Good thing Dr. Arnold didn't take the time machine to Trenton and warn *them*."

Ty shook his head. "That wouldn't have helped Benedict Arnold. He was still a Patriot at the time, would've hanged with the other rebel leaders if the British had won so early in the war."

"Why does Crazy Arnold hate Washington so much?"

"George got the glory, while Benedict had to run away to England in shame."

"Oh, I get it. But if Arnold helps that André guy, nobody will know Benedict's a traitor. So why don't we just *tell* someone? We can find some soldiers and tell them what Benedict's planning."

"Who'll believe us? I'm a Brit—a Tory. And you're—" He stopped himself.

She frowned. "You can say it—I'm just a black servant."

He flushed. "That's not what I was going to say."

"But it's true. Here, I'm no one. Nothing."

"You're *not* nothing! You're going to be a rich lawyer someday, or—or something. How many servants can say that?"

"Yeah, if we ever get out. Or back. Or—whatever."

He took her hands, looked into her eyes. "I'll get you home, Kristi. I will. I promise."

***

Hours later, pops sounded through the trees, like a string of firecrackers. Ty woke and sat up, strained to listen, but heard nothing but the gurgling river. The birds weren't even chirping.

The sky was paling to gray. Thick fog weaved between the trees. The fire had cooled to gray ash and the mosquitoes were back in Kamikaze mode. He slapped one feasting on his neck, then pulled his blanket over his head.

Then a thunderous boom ripped the air.

Stephen was up instantly, dragging them by their arms. "Get under the wagon!"

Kristi blinked. "What's happ—"

Pop, Pop, Pop

Fiery flashes erupted through the fog.

They scrambled under the wagon as six men in blue coats rushed into the clearing, pursued by musket fire, more pops and flashes through the fog. A mini-ball smacked into the ground a foot from Ty's head, spraying his face with dirt. Stephen pulled him further under, shielded him with his thin body.

The bluecoats scattered, and suddenly, the trees were swarming with red. The first five or six British soldiers stopped to kneel and fire around the wagon. They fell back and another group raced past.

Boom—Boom—Boom

The cannon shot rattled the trees, showering leaves like rain. Then, as quickly as they'd come, the soldiers were gone, the trees still. The pop of musket fire faded in the distance.

TEN

"That was awesome!" Kristi scrambled from under the wagon and looked up the road. Dozens of golden spotlights streamed through holes in the canopy of the trees. The smell of gun powder had dissipated. The birds had begun singing again, accompanied by the gurgle of the river. The clearing was so peaceful, so serene, it seemed impossible two fighting armies had just torn through. Her heart still pattered like a drummer. "A *real* battle, right in front of us. *Real* guns. *Real* soldiers. Incredible."

"Real *danger*," Stephen said, laying one hand on her shoulder. His face was pale, drawn, like he'd aged another twenty years. "You all right?"

She grinned. "Not a scratch."

"And you, lad?"

Ty rubbed watery eyes. "Got a bit of dirt in my eye, but I'm whole."

"Good. Come on, we have to get away from the road in case they come back."

Kristi gulped. "*Back?*"

Stephen approached Belle and Foxe, who were tied to trees on the other side of the wagon. The horses were stamping and snorting, apparently not finding the battle as exciting as Kristi had. Ty joined him. After a bit of coaxing and many soothing words, they calmed the frightened beasts and hitched them to the wagon. Kristi climbed onto the bench and took the reins while Stephen and Ty led the horses into the trees, bouncing the wooden wheels over fallen branches and exposed roots. They stopped in another small clearing a hundred yards in and waited; sweating, slapping mosquitoes, breakfasting on hard bread and harder dried beef.

After hours that seemed to drag into days, Kristi heard the faint thump of drums. The beats grew louder until the first red coats showed on the road. Two boys with sunburned faces and sandy blonde hair, looking no older than Kristi and Ty, headed the column, beating their drums with a steady *rat-tat-rat-tat-rat-tat-rat-tat.* Behind them rode two officers with gleaming white breeches, blood red coats, and shiny swords hanging in their scabbards. Then came the foot soldiers, hundreds of them, muskets propped on shoulders, marching two by two, dusty black boots rising and falling as one.

"Holy God," Kristi said. "So *many* of them!"

The procession seemed to take hours to pass. Toward the end, sandwiched between redcoats, tramped two-dozen men in ragged uniforms, medleys of patched blues, grays, and browns. Some wore boots, others moccasins. Still others were barefoot. None had muskets and all trudged with heads low, looking miserable.

"Prisoners?" Ty asked.

Stephen nodded.

"What's going to happen to them?" Kristi asked.

"Probably headed for prison ships." Stephen sighed. "Horrid places where many will die of dysentery."

"Poor blokes," Ty said.

Kristi nodded, suddenly feeling guilty about her previous excitement at the battle.

They watched the remaining soldiers pass in silence. When the last red coats faded in the dust, Stephen led the wagon back onto the road and they continued, lurching along under the oppressive heat of the midday sun.

Sore rump forgotten, Kristi's head swiveled, scanning the trees and fields for signs of more Redcoats.

Before they'd gone half a mile, she saw a dark shape lying ahead in the road, like the carcass of a deer on the side of the highway. Three buzzards circled high above it.

"Don't look." Stephen put one arm around her, tried to shield her eyes.

She pushed him off. An icy chill ran up her spine. As they got closer, she saw a swarm of flies hovering around the body. Limp, lifeless legs stuck out, one twisted impossibly backwards. The soldier lay face down, the back of his white shirt stained with a splotch of red bigger than a basketball.

She heard a high, keening sound, and someone pulled her face into scratchy fabric; a strong arm held her shoulder. As the cry continued, deep, guttural, she realized it was her own voice. Stephen hugged her to his side, hand on the back of her head so she couldn't look back again.

"Shhhh," he said, stroking her hair.

After a few minutes, she wiped her eyes on his shirt and pushed herself up again. Her vision was clouded by tears, her throat raw. The relentless, beating sun made it feel two hundred degrees.

Ty took her hand. "You all right?"

She took a deep breath and nodded weakly. "Yeah, I think."

"There'll be more," Stephen said. "Maybe you should get in the back."

She shook her head, set her jaw. She wasn't going to be a stupid, *girly-girl* in front of them again.

The second body wore a red coat with shiny silver buttons and polished black boots. He lay on his back, face turned away. A blackened hole in his jacket above the left breast showed where the ball had gone in. Kristi shivered, but kept her cool.

As they bumped toward the third body, two buzzards took flight, leaving their find behind. He wore no coat, just a stained grayish shirt and brown breeches. His right arm was torn off at the shoulder, head lolled to the side, eyes open, staring.

Sour vomit burned the back of Kristi's throat. But she couldn't tear her gaze from the empty, black eyes.

She was suddenly dizzy. "I—I have to lie down."

Ty helped her over the bench. She sat back on a lumpy sack of potatoes and stared up at the empty blue sky. "All right?" he said.

She raked hands down her face. "How are you so calm?"

"Dunno."

"Did you see the—the bodies, the blood, the flies?"

He closed his eyes and nodded.

Just a few hours earlier she'd been thrilled at having witnessed a battle, eager to see another. Battles had always been the only interesting parts of her history classes. She'd loved the heroics in countless movies where the brave, selfless heroes had overcome certain death to defeat the bad guys.

But she'd never considered the *real* cost of bullets and cannons. For every war hero she'd heard of—every George Washington, Paul Revere, Nathaniel Greene—how many other men and boys had been left on the sides of roads, on bloody battlefields? Boys who'd never hug their parents again. Never marry, have children. Never taste the freedom they'd supposedly died for.

She closed her eyes, but still saw the black, empty stare of the soldier missing an arm, felt it down to her soul. She shook the image away, tried only to gaze ahead, but locked on another set of lifeless legs, dirty white tights and brown breeches, lying off to one side in the long grasses. Just as she ripped her gaze away, one leg twitched.

"*Stop!*" She grabbed Stephen's arm. "That one's alive!"

He hauled back on the reins and the horses danced and sidestepped. She and Ty jumped down before the wagon stopped moving.

She approached slowly. "Hello? Are you, um, ok?"

The man groaned. Stephen pushed past her, knelt, and turned him over. Like the other Continental, he wore no coat, just a bloused, bloodstained shirt. His face was filthy and he breathed in short, racking gasps. One shoulder of his shirt was soaked red.

"Get water and a blanket," Stephen ordered. Ty went back to the wagon and Kristi knelt on the other side of the wounded man.

Stephen laid a hand on the soldier's forehead. "What's your name, son?"

He coughed and winced. "Charles."

"I'm Stephen Haines. I'm going to take a look at your wound." He unbuttoned the shirt and pulled it down. The shoulder was a blackened, bloody mess.

Kristi closed her eyes, but took the man's hand. He squeezed weakly.

"How old are you, Charles?" asked Stephen as he probed around the wound.

"Sixtee—Ahhh!" Charles's grip on Kristi's hand strengthened until it threatened to break her fingers. He thrashed and kicked as if someone had driven a knife into the shoulder.

"Hold his legs," Stephen ordered.

Kristi pried her hand free, flexed some blood back into it, and held one leg down while Ty held the other.

"Sixteen, huh? Where you from?"

A sharp intake of breath. "B—Boston."

"Ah. A noble city." Stephen poured water over the oozing wound and wiped blood away with one corner of the quilt, revealing a quarter-sized hole. "You're lucky. The ball went clean through, missed your collarbone. We're going to get you up and into the wagon. Can you walk?"

He blinked, took a deep breath. "I—I believe so, sir."

Stephen tore a strip from the quilt and used it to tie the injured arm in a sling. Then he helped him to his feet, draped Charles's good arm over his shoulder.

Ty climbed into the back of the wagon and started stacking baskets of corn. He turned and shook his head. "Not enough room here for him to lie down."

Kristi climbed in to help. They ended up throwing two baskets of corn and three baskets of potatoes over the side. They reached down to pull Charles in, laying him flat on another quilt.

"Where's the rest of your unit?" Stephen asked.

"We were marching to Trenton when the bloody-backs ambushed us. What's left should be headed back to Morristown."

"All right, son. We'll get you there." Stephen touched Charles's forehead.

The boy closed his eyes again. "God, but it pains me."

Kristi and Ty stepped over the bench as Stephen climbed up. Kristi grabbed his arm and whispered, "Is he going to die?"

"Don't know. We have to get the wound properly cleaned before it becomes infected."

Her stomach turned as she looked at the wounded boy's dirty face and torn, bloody clothes. Sixteen—just a few years older than she was.

***

In the late afternoon, Charles began moaning. Kristi climbed in back and wiped his forehead with a rag dampened with water from a skin. His face was burning, soaked with sweat, yet he was shivering. He opened his eyes a few times, showing only whites. Once he looked up at her, as if puzzled, and said, "Mama?"

Just before dusk, as the mosquitoes arrived for their evening suckings, she spotted a farmhouse, its yard lined with torches. As the wagon drew near, three men stepped from the long grass on the side of the road.

"Halt!" They leveled long muskets. When Stephen drew up, two more men advanced on either side of the wagon.

"What business have you here?" one barked.

Stephen raised both hands. "A wounded boy. One of your own."

Another soldier took off his hat, revealing matted curly brown hair, and leaned in over the side. "It's Charlie!" He pushed his musket into Ty's hands and grabbed Charles's arm. "Darn it, boy. Thought we'd lost ya."

The leader lowered his musket. "Get him to the house."

The curly-haired soldier hung on the side of the wagon as they jostled up the drive. He had bright green eyes and a soft, round face dotted with pimples. "Name's Jonas. Where'd you find my cousin, girl?"

"Near the river," Kristi said. "He got shot in the shoulder."

"Ah, ain't no musket ball tough 'nough to take down Charlie-boy for long," he grinned. "I told 'em that when he went missin', but the colonel wouldn't let me go look. If the lobster-backs didn't get me, his mama shore woulda, if'n I'da gone home without 'im. I'm the one talked 'er into lettin' 'im join up."

The farmhouse was twice as big as Stephen's. A distance off sat a large barn and a paddock with at least twenty horses. Jonas jumped down before the wagon stopped and ran to the house, returning shortly with two other boys. They took the ends of the quilt like a stretcher and carried Charles into the house. Stephen followed.

Kristi looked around. The sickening feeling returned, stronger. Here, dozens of wounded men lay in the grass, moaning and writhing, calling out for water, for doctors, for their mothers.

"You there, girl." She flinched and looked up. A man on the front porch was leaning over a wounded man. His loose white shirt was splattered with blood. "Fetch some water."

"From where?" she asked.

"Well's 'round back. Be quick about it," he snapped.

Ty nodded. "Go. I'll see if I can help Stephen." He ran off into the house.

She found a bucket next to the porch and cranked the pump behind the house until it was full. When she got back, the man who'd sent her had already moved on to another soldier. She held the bucket out, but he shook his head. "Give it to them." He pointed to the wounded men in the yard.

She hesitated a moment, then grabbed a tin dipper from the porch and leaned over the first soldier. A young boy. His face was sallow, lips white, dry and cracked. Both arms were bandaged.

"Need a—a drink?"

His eyes fluttered open. She dipped some up and held it out. When he didn't reach for it, she knelt and poured a little into his mouth. He coughed, spraying her face. She wiped it on one sleeve, then lifted his head and raised the dipper to his lips.

"Thank you," he whispered, then lay back.

When she moved to the next one, she almost screamed. Bloody bandages covered a stump where the man's right leg should've been. But he was smiling. "Don't you fret, Miss. I can still dance with one good leg."

She smiled. "I'm sure you can. Uh—water?"

"Girl, I'm dryer than dust in a drought."

He sucked down two dippers full before she moved on. She spent the next hour moving from soldier to soldier, speaking a few words to each, helping them to drink. Each new wound gave her a fresh shock: shredded flesh, missing arms or legs, burned faces. She tried hard to push revulsion and fear aside, glad to give them even a few seconds of relief.

She'd crossed paths with Ty a couple times, but they'd only had time for tired nods. He looked pale as a zombie. His shirt was splattered with blood. What horrors had he seen inside the house? She didn't even want to imagine.

When she'd visited each man and boy in the yard, she started over.

The boy who'd coughed in her face the first time around lay still, as if sleeping. But when she knelt next to him and touched his shoulder, his head lolled to the side. His chest didn't rise and fall.

She gasped, pulled back as if she'd touched a burning iron, fought the tears forming in her eyes.

"His name was Johnny."

She spun, startled. Jonas was standing behind her, face grim, tired.

"Joined up a few months after me and Charlie-boy. Stepped off the farm took up a musket. Jus' fourteen years old."

"I can't do this!" Hot tears spilled over her cheeks. She dropped the bucket, slopping its contents on the ground, and covered her face. "I—I shouldn't be here."

Jonas touched her shoulder and smiled. "Can't give up yet, girl. Lot's o' hurtin' boys countin' on you."

She blinked, took a deep breath, then nodded.

Jonas winked and went back into the house.

After another deep breath, she picked the bucket up, returned to the pump to refill it, and continued, convincing herself the small comforts she brought these dying boys were worth her pain.

After more trips back to the well than she could count, she at last collapsed onto a bloodstained blanket, her shift too covered with other people's blood to even care. She just closed her eyes and fell asleep in seconds.

***

Ty *was* a zombie. He followed Stephen and the surgeon throughout the house as they helped wounded boys. *American* boys. It was weird. These blokes were fighting *his* countrymen. Should he hate them? What would they say if they found out he was British?

Yet these were the pained, wracked faces of mere boys—not enemies, not evil doers. Pity, not enmity, was all he felt. What did it matter who they fought for?

He knelt beside Charles, held his good arm as the surgeon, a whiskey-smelling old man with gnarled, shaky fingers, dug around in the hole in his shoulder with forceps. The surgeon confirmed that the musket ball had gone straight through without chipping bone. But Charles's shoulder was shredded in back where it had come out.

After cleaning the wound, the surgeon handed Ty a roll of white cloth and staggered out of the room. Stephen came up behind him and the two of them wrapped Charles's shoulder and laid him back to rest.

"Thank you," Charles groaned weakly.

Stephen nodded. After the boy's eyes fluttered shut, he turned to Ty. "Go help Kristi outside. You don't need to see any more of this."

Ty shook his head. "I'm fine. I want to help here."

"Then I'm proud to work beside you." Stephen clapped his shoulder and they followed the old surgeon into the next room.

The rest of the night, Ty helped bandage heads, arms, and legs. He smelled the sweet stink of burning of flesh as the surgeon used a glowing poker to cauterize a gaping hole in one man's thigh. He held the clenched hand of another soldier as the surgeon dug a long, scary looking bullet extractor into the man's stomach, heard him scream, felt the hand go limp, watched the head loll to the side, the chest stop rising and falling. The smells of blood and death filled his nose until he thought he'd never smell anything sweet again.

The hours stretched into a whole night. As Ty stood holding another man's arm, he fell asleep on his feet, teetering sideways, dangerously close to a small table lined with the surgeon's sharp, grisly instruments.

"Ty," Stephen said sharply.

He jerked awake and blinked heavily. "Sorry."

Stephen smiled. "Go get some rest."

"But I—"

"You've done enough. There'll be plenty more to do in the morning."

Ty nodded reluctantly, and left. He wanted to check on Charles again. The boy was sleeping peacefully. His forehead was warm, but not as hot as before.

Ty yawned and rubbed his eyes. He dipped a rag into a bucket, wrung out the pinkish water, and laid it across Charles's forehead. Heavy footsteps clomped up from behind. A grizzled man with a scar from chin to left ear stepped up beside him. His shirt was un-tucked, hanging to his thighs, sleeves rolled to his elbows. His right hand was wrapped like a club in white linen. Ty vaguely remembered wrapping it himself, hours earlier. Colonel Davis, he thought the fellow's name was. He'd been shot in the hand, had lost two fingers.

"God bless you for helping my men, son," the tall colonel said, voice tired, gravelly.

"Glad to be able to, sir," Ty said, then took a deep breath. "What happened?"

Davis sighed and leaned back against the wall. "I was to reinforce Trenton with two hundred men. Our scouts reported a clear road ahead, but the lobster-backs came out of nowhere. Ambushed us in a gully."

"Two hundred? But there's not fifty men here."

Davis pinched the bridge of his nose. "We held the devils off long as we could. When they rolled out the cannon, we had to retreat. They chased us for a few miles, picking us off one by one." He sighed and ran a finger the length of the livid scar.

"How'd you get that?"

"Makes me a pretty specimen, don' it?" He grinned. "A bayonet back at Saratoga nearly took off my head. But the ladies do like a dueling scar."

Ty gaped. "*Saratoga*. Do you know a man named Benedict Arnold?"

"General Arnold? Aye. I was twenty feet away when he took a ball to the hip."

"Really? What's he like?"

Davis shrugged. "Brave. Ambitious. Cockier than a man ought to be. He ignored the commander's orders, took us right into the belly of the beast. Turned the battle, though, he did. Word is General Washington's sent him to take command of West Point."

Ty tried not to sound too eager. "How far away is that?"

"About seventy miles, as the crow flies. The old man said you're heading there. We're leaving for Morristown in the morning. Don't fear—we shall get you that far."

"Thank you, sir."

The man bowed shortly. "I thank *you*, son, for your kind ministrations. I thank you again, for my men."

ELEVEN

For the trek to Morristown, Stephen had unloaded half the produce in the wagon in exchange for a handful of Continental notes. Ty rode in the back with Kristi, Jonas, and Charles, whose fever had broken with the dawn. The boy's face was ashen and he grimaced with every bump in the road, but he sat up against the boards, arm bandaged to his chest in a sling of red cloth.

The day had started hot, so humid Ty had felt he was trying to breathe through a sodden towel. But an hour into the ride, cooling winds blew in, bringing dark, billowing clouds that rumbled like boulders rolling down a mountain, blanketing the sky so that midday looked like dusk.

Ty knelt at the wagon's edge, scanning the trees and rocks for red coats.

"BOO!"

He jerked, startled.

Jonas's grinning face was hanging over his shoulder and the others were laughing. "Wha'cha lookin' for, boy?"

Ty sat back, face hot.

"Don' you worry about no bloody-backed nincompoops." Jonas spat over the side. "Split a lobster's shell and it's naught but pale slimy meat with no backbone."

Thunder cracked and Ty jumped again.

Charles frowned and touched his wounded shoulder. "Where you from, girl?" he asked Kristi.

She went rigid. "Ah. Well—we're, uh—"

"No, wait. Let me." Jonas grabbed her hands.

"Hey!" said Kristi. "What are you—"

"Here we go." Charles chuckled. "My cousin thinks he's a gypsy fortune teller. Go on, then—tell us her darkest secrets."

Jonas turned the hand over and ran one finger up to her elbow. "Yer no field hand, I'll vow. Never done no farm work with those soft hands, have ya?" He looked into her eyes and frowned. "You be a smart 'un, too. Bet you can even read. But you're far from home. Tryin' to find your family, ain't ya?"

She pulled the hand back and looked down, silent.

"I sure hope you find 'em, missy." He glanced at Ty. "Now you, boy."

Ty extended a hand, but Jonas pushed it down and cupped the sides of his face instead. He stared as if trying to figure a math problem. "Yer even farther from home, I'd swear to that."

Ty pulled his head back, looked away, flicked a splinter sticking from the side rail. What would they do to him if they knew he was British? Tar and feather him? Harass him as Jeffrey had? It suddenly occurred to him that Jeffrey had been exactly the type of American his British teachers had preached about. *Jeffrey* was the radical, self-serving prat. He looked at Jonas and Charles. Like the wounded boys he'd nursed the night before, they weren't the faces of radicals or unruly mob formers. They weren't the faces of bullies. Jeffrey was the *exception*, not the rule. He took a deep breath. "I'm from—from London."

"Ha! Thought you was a lobster spawn." Jonas jutted an accusatory finger into Ty's face. "You be spyin' on us then, boy?"

"No! No, I—"

Charles kicked at Jonas. "Leave 'em alone, nincompoop."

Jonas grinned. "I'm just havin' a bit of fun with ye. Can spot a spy a mile away, and you sure ain' one—don' have the shifty eyes. But yer tryin' to pick sides, ain' ya? Heard about us backwards yanks disobeyin' *His Majesty*. Now yer startin' to think maybe we *do* got a bone to pick." He winked. "How'm I doin'?"

Ty shrugged. "Not bad."

Jonas's lip curled. "So tell 'im, Charlie boy. Tell what *His Majesty* did to yer family. Tell 'im why we're fightin'."

Charles's face turned grim. He touched his shoulder again. "My father was a waterman, after his father and his father's father. Fishing's all the man ever knew and he was darn good at it; kept half the bellies in our village full of crab, codfish, and mackerel. Then *His Majesty* blockaded Boston Harbor. Within a week, the London bank come calling for the money he'd borrowed. Did the same to everyone in town who wasn't Tory. In Boston, my father and eldest brother joined some others protesting it. The lobsters called it a riot and arrested people. My father and brother were hauled off to a prison ship for carrying a placard. No charges, no trial. Eighteen months later the shell of my brother came home, skinny as a fence post. Our father—" His lip quivered. "He starved on the ship. They tossed his body into the river." His face hardened. "The lobsters don't want loyal subjects. They want beat-down servants. If we don't fight back, that's all we'll ever be."

Jonas smacked the rail. "No matter all their guns and cannons and warships. I'm gonna snap off their pincers and send 'em to the bottom of the sea!"

A chill prickled Ty's arms. Charles and Jonas weren't statistics in a history book. Not slave owners or smugglers. All they wanted was to be free. To *live.* He took a deep breath, let it out, smiled. They deserved that much. Didn't everyone?

Another bolt of lightning flashed. Thunder shook the air. The clouds let go their heavy burden, engulfing them in a curtain of fat raindrops.

***

The sky dumped buckets for two hours, saturating the wagon and the world around it. Howling wind whipped the trees, its roar only ever interrupted by thunder cracking like firing cannons. Ty huddled against the side, soaked to the bone.

The wagon lurched, then stopped suddenly. The horses jerked and snorted, pulling the reins taut, but they didn't move.

Stephen's curses rose over the wind. Ty leaned over and saw the back wheels were buried to the axels in mud.

"Going to have to push her out," Stephen called back.

"It's me and you, little limey," Jonas said, then hopped over the side.

"Great," Ty muttered. He kicked off his shoes and followed, meeting Jonas at the back of the wagon. "So we just push?"

"Yup."

The wind had died down a little. Stephen was yelling, encouraging the horses.

"Git 'er rockin'," Jonas said.

Ty tried to push, but his feet slipped on the mud as if it were sheer ice. Beside him, Jonas was almost horizontal, leaning a shoulder into the wagon and digging his feet in.

Ty turned, leaned his back against the wagon's gate, and planted his feet. The thick, slimy mud squished between his toes, sucked at his ankles like quicksand. He gritted his teeth and pushed. The wagon inched forward, back, forward, back, gaining a little momentum.

"Keep 'er goin'," Jonas yelled.

Ty timed the motion, forward, back, forward, back. He let the wagon roll back at him, crouched like a taut spring, then shot out, pushing with all his might. The wheels creaked and the wagon lurched. But Ty's feet slid from under him and he fell. The big wheels rolled back toward him. He floundered, unable to gain any purchase in the mud. Just before the wheel crushed him, Jonas grabbed his ankle and hauled him out of the way.

Ty let out a relieved breath and laid his head back in the mud. He tried to wipe rain from his eyes, but only caked his face with muck. "Th-thanks."

Jonas grinned and helped him up. "Almost 'ad us a limey hoe cake."

"I have an idea." Kristi kicked off her shoes and jumped down into the mud. "My brother used to go mud-bogging in his truck. He got stuck all the time."

"Mud-boggin'?" Jonas's forehead wrinkled. "You touched, girl? What'n providence is a truck?"

"Uh—never mind," she said quickly. "Just a sort of—wagon. Get some sticks and branches to shove under the wheels for traction."

She and Ty left Jonas staring quizzically and gathered sticks from under the surrounding trees.

"Seriously, Kristi," Ty whispered. "Mud-bogging? Are you bonkers?"

She grinned. "Maybe a little."

They returned with armloads and stuffed sticks and branches behind the back wheels, then made a path in front of them like a ramp. The three of them lined up behind the bed. Stephen snapped the reins and they got the wagon rocking again. Sticks popped as it lurched forward.

Careful to keep his feet under him, Ty bent and kept the pressure on. This time, the wagon didn't roll back. More branches snapped as it surged out of the mud hole.

Charles cheered.

"Well done, girl!" Stephen called back.

Kristi beamed.

"Well I'll be," Jonas said. "Whate'er mud-boggin' be, I'd swear it worked a treat!"

Ty grinned. Kristi took a handful of mud and squished it in his face. "Now who's bonkers?"

They both laughed and climbed back into the wagon.

***

Black clouds gave way to stringy white ones with spatters of blue sky interspersed. Ty rode on the bench next to Stephen, still scrapping gritty muck from his face and arms. As they crested a long, low hill, thousands of white tents lay spread out before them, speckling the wet green grass like grains of salt.

Ty gaped. "Is this Morristown?"

"Largest Continental force in the colonies," Stephen said.

Men moved about, hanging out rain-soaked clothes, lighting fires. One with a gray ponytail and three-cornered hat rode through the camp on a huge white gelding. His smart blue coat and white knee-breeches looked freshly washed and pressed, the brass buttons shiny. A sword with an ornate, carved hilt hung in a scabbard at his hip. A black man rode beside him, also smartly dressed in tan coat and breeches.

Ty's breath caught. "Is that—I mean it can't be. Can it?"

Stephen grinned. "That's him, all right."

"Kristi, get up here!"

She leaned over the bench. "What's wrong?"

"Look! You know who that is?"

Her eyes widened. "That's—*oh my God*—George Washington!"

"Amazing!" Ty said. "The general himself in flesh and blood."

"Cool!" She gasped. "We have to get his autograph. It'll be worth *millions*."

Stephen shook his head. "We've got more important things to worry about. Only three days left to get to Tarrytown and we're still fifty miles and a river away. On muddy roads, we'll never make it with the wagon. We'll have to leave it behind."

"But your harvest," Ty protested.

"Martha and I will manage. We've been through rougher times. More important that we put another ten miles behind us before nightfall. Think you can handle that pace?"

Kristi raised her eyebrows. "Don't have much choice, do we?"

He patted her head. "Afraid not, m' girl."

***

To Ty, the camp was more like the London slums than a military stronghold. An invisible musty cloud of sweat, rank body odor, and manure hung over everything. They passed a pen of bleating goats and the stench intensified. The tents were thin as bed sheets, frayed, with more holes than Swiss cheese. Hacking coughs seemed to come from each one. Most of the soldiers they saw were either skinny old men with long, gray beards or hungry-eyed boys who couldn't have been more than fifteen or sixteen, like Jonas and Charles.

Ty shook his head. How could such a rag-tag force ever defeat the great British army? It explained the scorn his teachers still held two hundred-thirty years later. A gang of farmers and blacksmiths, old men and kids, had humiliated all of England.

Stephen passed them strips of dried meat.

"Thanks," Ty said and tried to bite into one. It was like trying to chew a shoe-sole dipped in salt. "Um—what is it?"

"Goat."

Kristi pretended to gag, but chomped away nonetheless.

"When do we leave?" Ty asked.

"Now."

Kristi looked up. "Can we find Jonas and Charles to say goodbye?"

Stephen shook his head. "The fewer questions we have to answer, the better. We need to go. There's a long road in front of us."

Stephen rode Foxe, while Kristi and Ty shared Belle. A cold drizzle started up again as soon as they left. They made the ten miles Stephen had hoped. When they stopped at last to camp, Ty walked bowlegged, his rump and legs all but howling from the miles on horseback. It was too wet to light a fire, so they wrapped in sodden, squelchy blankets and lay on the soggy ground.

The next morning at sunrise the sky was clear and the birds chirped merrily. They rode throughout the day without incident and stopped next to a large lake at dusk to camp again.

Kristi dropped a log onto the fire and sparks flew up. "So, how much farther now?"

Ty opened the journal to the maps and Stephen pointed. "We're here, a couple miles from the Hudson. We'll cross here at Nyack and head south to Tarrytown." He drew his finger along the route.

Ty leafed through the journal by the light of the fire. "André is supposed to be captured the morning of the twenty-third."

"That's the day after tomorrow," Stephen said.

"So what if we can't find Arnold before that," Kristi asked.

Stephen sighed. "I don't know."

***

Kristi lay awake, listening to the crickets, unable to sleep for thinking about all that had happened and was to happen. Charles had lost everything, even his father. The thought of her dad starving on a prison ship, or anywhere, made her blood run cold. But after what he'd done to the family, would she still fight for him as hard as Charles?

She sighed, turned over, and gazed into the dying embers. Dad had always lectured her about making sacrifices. When she'd complain about hating school, he'd point out that her grandfather hadn't even been allowed to go to school with white kids. That her great-great-great-grandfather had been a slave who wasn't even allowed to read or write.

Her lip curled. So then what did *he* do? Throw his whole, real family away. Before she'd left for prep school, she'd heard mom crying in her room each night. How dare he lecture anyone about *sacrifice*!

She kicked a stone into the embers. Mama, the old slave who'd helped her escape—she knew sacrifice. All the slaves did. They were *owned*, like livestock. They couldn't go to classes or live in a big house like she had.

Her stomach dropped.

The way she'd acted at school, causing trouble, trying to get kicked out, was like spitting in their faces. And she'd been so proud of her *rebellion*. Like she'd had the right to act the brat just because she didn't want to be there.

She set her jaw. They all deserved better. She owed it to Mama. To her grandparents and her mother. She'd prove she could handle a stupid school, happy or not. Then she'd tell her dad how she felt; yell and scream. Show *him* what he'd sacrificed: her love.

***

It seemed only minutes later when Ty shook her awake. She grumbled, dragging herself up, and slogged through the camp. "No sleep," she muttered. "My stupid butt hurts. I think I'm getting mildewed. And here we go again, stale bread and salted goat leather to eat. *Awesome!*"

She took her time getting ready, still grumbling, while Stephen and Ty waited. Only halfway to Nyack did she remember her promise by the fire the night before, and feel ashamed.

They paused at the top of a long hill to look down at the wide gray Hudson River snaking through a lush, green valley. A peninsula like a hand with an extended finger jutted into the river.

Stephen led them down the slope. They stopped at a wood-slatted shack on one bank. "I'll arrange for the ferry. You two stay here."

They swung down, kicked off their shoes, and stepped into the ankle-deep water. A flat-bottomed ferry, weighed down by a wagon, six horses, and six men, had just launched from the landing, pulled across on a rope stringing across both shores.

"Just missed it," she said. "Wonder how long 'til the next one."

Ty's mouth dropped open.

She squinted at him. "What's wrong with you?"

His hand shook as he pointed. Standing at the back of the just-departing ferry stood a tall, skinny man in a brown suede jacket. His bald, white head gleamed in the sun.

She gasped. "That's Dr. Arnold!"

TWELVE

Kristi swore and chucked a stone into the river. "It's my fault! If I hadn't loafed around and taken my good ol' time this morning, we could be out of this freaking century and home by now!"

"Don't beat yourself up," Ty said. "You couldn't have known he'd be here."

Stephen stroked his beard. "Did he see either of *you*?"

She huffed and plopped onto the bank. "Don't think so."

"Who were the others?" Ty said. "Could they be helping him?"

Stephen nodded. "It's possible. He's going to need help."

"Great!" She kicked the water. "Probably some stupid British wankers. Oh—sorry, Ty."

He grinned. "That's just what I was going to say."

"We'll stick to the plan," Stephen said. "If we can find Arnold in Tarrytown tonight, we'll find a way to steal the time machine. But André comes through tomorrow morning. If we don't find Arnold before then, we'll just have to go to the crossroads to warn the soldiers. If we're lucky, he'll come to us."

Ty raised an eyebrow. "Lots of *ifs* in there."

"Don't I know it, boy."

***

It was past midday when the ferry returned to take them across the river. A cool breeze blew across the river. The sun glittered like thousands of tiny diamonds across the water's rippled surface. Kristi stood at the edge of the ferry, still fuming. It didn't matter what Ty said. It *was* her fault they'd missed Dr. Arnold on the other side of the river. She should be home, putting history where it should be: long behind her. But no, she'd pouted and whined all morning, and now they had to keep chasing their crazy teacher.

Once they reached the far bank, they headed south. After an hour, they came upon a narrow crossroad in the woods.

Stephen pulled up and flipped through the journal again. "This is where André should try to come through. Tarrytown's another mile down the road. Come on."

He led them another hundred yards past the crossroads, then swung down and led Foxe off the road, up the hill. Kristi and Ty dismounted and followed. They crested the hill and went down the other side until they reached a small, level clearing.

"Stay here and wait for me," Stephen said. "No fires."

"*Wait*? What do you mean?" Ty said. "We're going with you."

"It's too risky."

"But you might need help," Kristi said. "We can cause a distraction, or—"

"No. If Arnold sees either of you, we may lose our only chance. I can get in and look around without causing a stir."

"I don't like it," Ty said.

"Sorry, but that's how it's got to be. If I'm not back by sundown, head to the river and find some Continentals. Tell them about Benedict Arnold and André."

"No!" Ty said. "We can't just—"

"He's right, Ty." Kristi touched his arm.

"But—"

She grabbed his wrist. "Think about it. If Arnold sees us before we have the time machine, he'll sic his men on us and—" A chill ran up her spine. "And give me over to a slave-catcher."

He opened his mouth to argue, then shook his head. "Fine!" He turned and kicked a small stone down the hill.

"I'll be back before nightfall," Stephen said.

"Just be careful," Kristi said.

"You too. No fires." He tipped his hat, led Foxe back up the hill, waved, and disappeared over the crest.

Kristi tied Belle to a tree.

Ty paced, then kicked a hollowed log. "This is so unfair of Stephen! *We* should be going after Arnold."

She laughed.

"What are you so chuffed about?" he snapped.

"If *I* have to calm *you* down now, we're in big trouble."

He took a deep breath and let it out slowly. "Quick, say something rash so I can redeem myself."

"Okay, how about we sneak into town, jump the first two soldiers we find, go all ninja on them and steal their guns. Then we'll find Crazy Arnold and force him at gunpoint to give us the time machine."

He grinned. "Sounds like a great scheme. Let's go!"

She punched his shoulder. "Wanker!" They laughed, then sat on a log and swatted mosquitoes for a while.

"So, you've told me all about the war and what Benedict's trying to do. But what made him go bad, anyway? Why'd he turn against his friends?" Kristi asked.

"It's complicated, I think," Ty said. "I guess he never got the credit he thought he deserved. He was a hero at Saratoga, almost got killed—but the commander didn't even mention him in the bloody report."

"How do you know all of this stuff?"

He shrugged. "Lots of reading time when you're hiding out from bullies in strange places."

She frowned. "Ok. I'll give you a new rash plan. When we get back home—to our time—I'm going to punch Jeffrey in his fat freaking nose."

"And now I suppose you expect me to say, '*No, no—it's not worth it*'. Hmmm." He tapped his chin. "Instead, think I'll pin his arms for you. Then we'll go after my step-dad."

She jumped up and threw a haymaker. "Take that, pizza face!"

"He's out!" Ty yelled, waving his arms.

She raised her arms in victory and danced in a circle. They laughed some more, then plopped back down on the log.

"Tell me more about good ol' Bennie Arnold," she said. "Know your enemy, right?"

"After Saratoga, Congress put him in charge of Philadelphia. He made some powerful chums and married the daughter of a rich Tory. But he made enemies too. The Governor of Pennsylvania thought Benedict was misusing government notes and demanded Washington bring him up on charges. When Washington didn't defend him to Congress, Arnold took it as another slight to his honor. Maybe he *was* stealing. His wife was from a rich family, and he couldn't have had much money left, so maybe that's when he started selling secrets. He figured the British would win sooner or later, and wanted to be on the winning side."

She frowned. "So why'd Washington still trust him?"

"They were only rumors at the time and I guess Washington didn't believe another gentlemen was capable of such things. You know, bloody honor and all that. Arnold convinced Washington to give him command of West Point, then schemed with André to turn it over to the British. If Dr. Arnold isn't able to interfere, Washington will be making a surprise visit to West Point when André is captured, but Benedict will escape on horseback before Washington hears about the spy. By the time Washington pieces it all together, Arnold will be on a British ship bound for New York."

"Ha!" She shook her head. "And Dr. Arnold wants to make that loser a hero."

***

Hours later, as the sun was dropping below the trees, Ty's agitation rose again. He paced, kicking a path through the leaves, mind racing. Kristi had tried distracting him with talk of school, the war, even farming, but he couldn't think past the sinking in his stomach. Something had gone wrong with Stephen. He could *feel* it. At last he snapped a small branch over one knee. "That's it! I'm going after Stephen."

"But we promised to wait."

"Until sundown. Well, it's down and I'm going. You stay here in case he comes back."

She gaped. "No way, limey!"

"It's safer. You're black, remember. You'll stick out more, and—"

"Don't tell me what I am, Ty! You're British, *remember*. We *both* stick out, so don't act so high and mighty!"

"That's not what I meant."

"I don't care what you meant!" She balled her fists. "I'm *not* waiting here alone."

"All right, all right. Calm down. We'll both go, then." He looked down at her clenched fists and chuckled. "You weren't going to cosh me, were you?"

She raised an eyebrow. "Guess now we'll never know. What do we do with Belle?"

Ty scratched his head, then hit upon an idea. "We can hobble her and let her graze. Stephen showed me how a few weeks ago."

"*Hobble?*" Her face twisted. "You wanna *break her leg*? That's horrible! We can't do that!"

Ty laughed. "You big city girls don't know anything." He dug in the saddlebag and brought out a long leather strap. "I'll tie this to both her front legs. She'll be able to get around and graze, but can't go too far." He stepped back and thought through the steps Stephen had taught him. He held it in front of her face, then rubbed her nose with it.

"What are you doing?"

"Showing her the hobble, so she doesn't go nutty when I strap it on her legs." He stroked her face and neck. "All right girl, this won't hurt. Promise." He strapped one front leg. She snorted and lifted it. Ty moved to the side in case the mare kicked, but she didn't. He stroked her neck again. "Good girl!" He strapped her other front leg and tightened. Belle snorted again and stepped back a little. Ty grabbed her head and rubbed his cheek against her face. "Shhhhh, girl. I'm done. I'm done. You're safe."

He stepped back and watched her. She stumbled a few times, but soon got the hang of the hobble.

"All right," Ty said. "Let's go."

They left Belle and made their way down to the road, then tramped alongside it, keeping to the trees until they came to a clearing and a town.

"Is this Tarrytown?" Kristi asked.

"Must be."

Torches and lamps lighted the street corners. Only a few men on horseback and a couple of carriages were out on the street. Most buildings had darkened first floors and candles in second story windows. Every third structure seemed to be an inn or tavern, with men coming and going in steady streams.

"I guess we check the taverns," Ty said.

Kristi went to the side window of the closest one. Ty went through the front door, where he ran right into a round-bellied man, a disturbing combination of Santa Claus and Blackbeard.

"Wha'cha doin' in here, boy?"

"I—I'm looking for my uncle, sir."

Santa Beard spun him by the shoulders and shoved him back outside. "Keep clear o' here till ye can grow a beard."

Ty turned back. "Please sir, I only want—"

"Run home to your mammy afore I give you a thrashin'!" The big man slammed the door.

Ty returned to Kristi, grinning sheepishly. "So...*that* didn't work."

Kristi shook her head. "No, *that* was stupid. I swear, Ty. You're supposed to be the leveled headed one, not—"

He grabbed her arm and pulled her into the shadowy alley next to the tavern.

"Hey! What're you doing?"

"Shhh—look!"

Dr. Arnold was riding up the street on an ash-gray quarter horse. Two somber men accompanied him, both on mules. One was so fat, his mule's legs trembled with every step.

Kristi squeezed Ty's hand. "It *is* him."

"Come on," Ty said after the men had passed. They followed, staying in the shadows of buildings, ducking behind lampposts.

Arnold and the others stopped in front of a boxy white tavern with candles lighting the two front windows. Ty could almost hear the fat man's mule sigh with relief as he dismounted. Arnold lifted a leather bag hung on the saddle horn and the men went inside.

"Where's Stephen?" Kristi whispered.

"I guess we watch the door now and hope he shows up."

They hid in a stinking alley full of garbage and piles of horse manure and watched, jumping up each time the tavern door banged open. After a long while, Arnold emerged again with the two men. He didn't have the bag. Arnold led the men up the street and the trio ducked down an alley.

"Let's go!" Ty pulled Kristi across the street and through the tavern's doorway door before she could protest.

They entered a long dim room with half a dozen rough plank tables and benches. Three bearded, gruff-looking men, each with pewter tankards, sat at separate tables. None looked up. An old man with a wrinkled, weathered face emerged from a door in the back.

Ty took a deep breath and stepped up to him. "Good evening, sir. My uncle sent me to fetch his bag."

The man frowned. "What uncle is that?"

"Mister Arnold. Xavier Arnold. He's staying at this tavern, sir. He forgot his bag when he left."

The old man narrowed his eyes at Kristi. "And who be the darkie?"

Ty shot her a glance. "She's our—our servant. But Uncle doesn't trust her alone with his purse, you see." He could almost feel Kristi's glare boring into the back of his head and motioned behind his back with one hand, hoping she took the hint.

The old man's scowl cleared. He finally nodded. "Aye, then. Up the stairs, second chamber on your left."

"Thank you, sir," Ty said. "We'll only be a moment."

As they rushed up the stairs, Kristi punched his shoulder. "Can't trust the *servant* with his purse?"

His face heated. "Sorry. First thing I could think of."

"Whatever." They stopped at the second plank door. "How'd you know Arnold would use his real name, by the way?"

"Egomaniac like him, what other name would he use?" He grabbed a candle from a wall sconce in the hall and they pushed inside. Arnold's room was about the size of a modern walk-in closet with a high narrow bed, small chest of drawers, and a flowered china pitcher and washbasin. "Watch by the door."

The chest of drawers was empty, so he bent to look under the bed. "It's not here."

"Has to be." She left the door and knelt beside him. "Maybe the guy told us the wrong room." She leaned to look, too, and one of the boards under her hand shifted. "Hey!" She pried it up with her nails, revealing the leather bag.

"*Brilliant!*" He hugged her neck, then dug through the bag. At last, he frowned and upended it. A linen shirt, a small leather coin purse, and two flints clattered to the floor. "Look down in the hole."

She felt around, then shook her head. "Nothing here. He must've—"

"Looking for this, kids?"

Dr. Arnold stood in the open doorway, face like a smirking jack-o-lantern in the dancing light of the candle he held. He pulled open his vest to reveal the time machine.

THIRTEEN

"**G et off me, you fat turd!**" Kristi kicked at the ankles of the man who'd dragged her out of the tavern, across the street, and into a low stone building with tiny windows. She fought all the way through a small room with only two tables. He opened a door, revealing a narrow flight of stairs leading down into darkness.

"Quit yer squirmin'."

She braced her feet on either side of the doorframe. The fat man yanked and she flew forward, skinning her knees on stone steps as he pulled her into the darkness. Half-way down, he hefted her over one shoulder and carried her like a sack, then tossed her through an opening onto a hard-packed dirt floor. She couldn't see anything in the dark, but felt Ty shoved in on top of her, then heard a heavy door slam with a loud clank.

She jumped up felt for the door, finding cold strips of metal. "Let us out!"

A minute later Arnold descended the stairs, holding a lantern that sent queer shadows dancing on the walls. They were in some type of holding cell, but instead of bars, like in the old movies she'd seen, the door was flat strips of crisscrossed iron with rectangular holes only a few inches high and wide. The two captors, one fat with a face like a stubbly hog, the other's dirt streaked with an eye patch, stepped aside.

"Arrest *him*!" She reached through and pointed at Arnold. "He's the traitor!" The hog-faced man gave her hand a stinging slap. "OWW!"

Arnold tsked. "Afraid you won't find any rebel sympathizers down here. These constables know which way the winds of revised history blow."

A hand clasped her shoulder from behind. She shrieked, then rounded on the figure, fists raised. A drawn, ghostly face with a white beard glowed in the light of the lantern. "Oh— Stephen!" She threw her arms around him. "What're you doing here?"

He hugged her, then stepped back and cradled her face. "Did they hurt you?"

"No, just some scrapes. What happened?"

"Ahh, such a touching reunion." Arnold pretended to wipe a tear. "Stevie here thought I wouldn't recognize him, being as he's old as dirt. Tsk, tsk. The years have *not* been kind, friend." He shook his head. "When I caught the old boy snooping, I knew you two wouldn't be far behind." He turned to the fat constable. "So what have we here? A spy, a thief, and a runaway slave?"

The fat man chuckled. "That be the score by my count, yer honor."

"We're not spies. And we didn't steal anything!" Kristi snapped.

"Don't deny it, girl," Arnold said. He produced the journal, which the skinny one had taken from Ty. "Then how did you get a journal with my name and notes? Confess and maybe you'll avoid the gallows."

"Mayhap," The fat constable said with a nasty, rotten-toothed grin. "Then again, a good hangin' is fair entertainment." The skinny one laughed as he clapped a rusty padlock on the door. Then the two constables stomped up the stairs.

Kristi gripped the rusted iron grate. "You can't do this to us!"

Arnold raised his eyebrows. "You've done it to *yourselves*. Shouldn't have meddled in matters you don't understand."

"What do you think you're doing?" she cried. "We know about John André and Benedict Arnold."

"It's not *meddling*, my dear. I'm correcting one of history's greatest wrongs."

Ty crossed his arms. "You're too late, mate. We've told everyone at Morristown about Benedict Arnold. George Washington *himself* will be waiting for André in the woods."

Arnold's face fell for a split second. Then he snorted. "Do you think I'm an idiot?"

"Yeah!" Kristi said. "A great *big* idiot!"

He glared. "This place would already be swarming with rebel troops if you had. Not a broken-down old farmer and a couple prep-school brats. No, Washington is on his way to West Point. And in three days' time, British forces will trap him like the bilge rat he is."

"Think of what you're proposing here, Xavier," Stephen said. "Without Washington, the revolution will fail. There'll be no United States."

"And my dear Grandpa Arnold will be a savior, honored by the crown, and will regain his rightful position in the aristocracy."

"But you're helping a traitor!" Ty said.

"Watch your tongue, boy! Maybe the gallows are too good. A prison ship would be the perfect place for the likes of you. Cozy, I hear. Lots to eat—if you don't mind cockroaches and rats."

Stephen pulled Ty back. "They've done nothing wrong, Xavier. You brought them here. Let them go, and I'll confess."

"No!" Kristi grabbed his arm. "You can't."

"Very noble, Stevie-boy. But the rich brat should have thought of that before she blew up my desk."

Kristi rolled her eyes. "It was just a Pull-Snap, you big baby."

Ty stepped in front of her. "Dr. Arnold. You don't have to do this."

"What do you care? It's your British countrymen these rebel swine are harassing." His head cocked, eyes narrowed. He muttered, "Your countrymen...," then rubbed his chin. "Hmm. I could use a witness to my triumphs. One who doesn't believe in all this revolutionary nonsense. I could use *you*, boy. No reason to rot here with them."

Ty's jaw dropped. "What?"

"Swear allegiance to me and we'll remake history together."

Ty looked as if he would be sick. Kristi touched his arm. "Do it, Ty. Save yourself at least." She took a deep breath, past the ache in her throat. "It's okay. We'd understand."

Arnold leaned closer. "What'll it be, m'boy? It's a great oppor—"

Ty spat in his face. Arnold stumbled back, face twisted in rage. "You idiotic limey TWIT! You'll hang for that!"

He grabbed the lantern and stomped up the stairs, leaving them in total darkness.

***

Kristi rolled over on the dirt floor and rubbed her neck. Had she slept? How long had they been trapped in this stinking dungeon? Minutes? Hours? Days? In the dark, with no windows, she couldn't tell. Time torture, again. At one point, the hog-faced man came down to throw a few hunks of hard bread at them. But who knew how long ago that had been.

"Where are you guys?" she whispered.

"Over here," Ty called from one corner.

"Any idea what time it is?"

"Don't know."

"You think André has come through yet?"

Stephen didn't answer.

A heavy door scraped open and daylight filtered down the stairs. Footsteps clomped down. Stephen grabbed her arm and whispered, "Follow my lead, you two."

The fat man hung a lantern on a hook. "Mornin', rats. Getting' the gallows ready. Town's abuzz. Yer all invited." He laughed and threw half a moldy loaf into the dirt.

Stephen picked it up and took a huge bite. He seemed to swallow hard, then gagged and clutched at his throat.

"*Stephen?*" Kristi grabbed his arm as he sank to his knees.

Ty grabbed the other arm. "He's choking!"

Now she couldn't tell if he was faking, or if his plan had gone horribly wrong. She smacked his back.

"Ah, no you don't!" The fat man unlocked the cell and stepped inside. "You ain't robbin' the hangman of his fun. Into the corner, filthy spawn." He shoved Kristi and Ty to the side, then hauled Stephen up by his collar. "I got just the trick." He balled one meaty fist and drew it back, readied to punch Stephen in the gut. He never got the chance. The old farmer suddenly lunged, slamming his forehead into the fat man's face. The constable let go and staggered back, cursing, gripping his nose.

"*Go!*" Stephen yelled and the three of them rushed out.

Ty slammed the door, then looked up, eyes frantic. "Where's the lock?"

The fat man laughed and wiped blood on his sleeve. "Looking for this, ratling?" He held up the padlock, his ring of skeleton keys hanging from it. "Get back in here so I can pound ye bloody."

Stephen pushed Ty away and leaned hard against the door. "Run!"

Ty hesitated. "What about you?"

The fat man shoved at the door, pushing Stephen back a few inches.

"Get out of here!" Stephen yelled. "Go!"

Kristi grabbed Ty's hand. She dragged him up the stairs and into the small office. The skinny man wasn't there. "No, wait!" Ty turned back. "We can't leave Stephen!"

This time, Kristi hauled him through the front door. "We'll come back for him—after we stop Arnold."

Outside, the sun was fully up. They raced through the streets, then across a cornfield, until they reached the woods, then stayed off the road until they found the crossroads and went up the hill. They found Belle in the clearing where they'd left her.

Kristi doubled over, panting. Her side felt like it was being ripped open.

"Now what?" Ty gasped.

Four muffled pops echoed from over the hill. Kristi forgot the stabbing pain in her side. "We're too late!"

They raced back up the hill and looked down. Three men in rough suede jackets knelt in the middle of the road, aiming long muskets up the hill.

Another round of shots sent plumes of smoke rising from the trees in front of them. Dirt kicked up around the exposed militiamen. They shot back, but were firing blindly at the hidden ambushers.

"They're sitting ducks!" she gasped. As if they'd heard and agreed, the militiamen scattered, clearing the road. She scanned the hill. "Where's Arnold?"

"Hiding like a rat, I'd wager," Ty said. "Come on."

They zigzagged down the hill, keeping trees between them and the skirmish.

"Look," Ty said when they were halfway down. He pointed and she saw Arnold's men. There were four of them spread in a semi-circle above the crossroads, two with muskets propped between branches of trees, two lying flat on their stomachs, firing from under large, thick bushes. "The Patriots don't stand a chance."

"Is one of them Arnold?" she asked.

"Can't tell—wait. There!"

A tall figure in a brown vest was posted thirty yards behind the semi-circle, hiding in the crevice between two boulders. He stuck his head up for a few seconds at a time, but ducked at the crack of each musket—even those fired by his own men.

"Told ya he'd be hiding like a rat," Ty said.

They crept on down the hill, moving between trees, and crouched behind a boulder ten feet from Arnold. Ty held up his fingers: *One...Two...THREE.*

He jumped on Arnold's back and the teacher staggered sideways. Kristi was on him then, too, wrapping her arms around his waist, biting his ear. Arnold screamed and cracked the side of her head with an elbow. She crumpled and fell off. The trees above her twirled in slow, hazy circles. The noise of the skirmish grew muffled, as if she was hearing it all under water.

Arnold grabbed Ty in a bear hug and squeezed. Kristi blinked heavily to slow the spinning. She turned her head to look down the hill. Through the trees, she saw a man on a brown horse galloping toward the crossroads. *André!* Arnold's men were peppering the trees with musket fire, keeping the militiamen pinned down.

"Somebody stop him!" she croaked.

But André sped through the pass unmolested and disappeared down the road, leaving a trail of dust.

"*Ha!*" Arnold threw Ty down and danced a jig. "I've done it! I've done it! *I've done it!*"

Ty closed his eyes, looking sick. Kristi rubbed her still woozy head. "So...what about...us?" she slurred.

Arnold looked down, as if just remembering them. He waved a hand. "You two can hang—as a runaway slave and a spy—for all I care. I've got history to make." He pulled the time machine from his jacket and bent the gleaming metal rod into a circle. Dirt and leaves swirled, as if he stood in the eye of a tornado. He held the flashing halo above his head, beaming like a toddler on Christmas morning.

"Ty!" She dragged him up. They braced against the wind and flying leaves and sticks. Then, just as Arnold lowered the time machine, Kristi grabbed his sleeve. She and Ty both screamed, slingshotting off with Arnold through a blur of swirling light and roaring wind.

***

Ringing bells jarred Kristi's head. Tears blurred her vision. Her nose picked up a musty scent, like a dank, mildewed basement. She pressed both hands to her head until the ringing subsided, blinking, trying to see where she was.

In a dim room, surrounded by crumbling cardboard boxes and stacks of graffiti-carved desks strung with dusty cobwebs thick as pulled cotton. She took a deep breath, sneezed, and rolled over, bumping into Ty. He groaned and his eyes fluttered open.

"You okay?" she whispered.

136

"Think so. Ugh! Where are we?"

"I don't know. It looks like—" she stopped and covered her mouth. "Hey! I think we're back at the school."

Ty shot up to look around. "But where's the lab?" The laptops, the flat screen, the office—they were all gone. An inch of dust covered everything, as if no one had been down there in years. "Where's Arnold?"

As if in answer, a muffled sound of miserable retching echoed through the junk. They wove through stacks and piles to find the man leaning against one wall, face buried in his hands. The time machine, its lights dark, lay on the floor beside him.

"Arnold!"

The teacher gasped as Ty tackled him into a stack of boxes. Kristi jumped out, grabbed the time machine, and ran for the door. Ty was up and behind her a second later.

They took the steps two at a time and burst into the school's main hallway. It was deserted, and looked as though it had been for a long, long time. The linoleum floor was cracked, caked with dust. Locker doors were ripped off or hanging by one hinge. The ones that remained were dented, rusted, as if someone had taken a bat to them, long ago. Classroom doors hung crookedly, their windows shattered. Wires hung through missing tiles in the ceiling like vines in a jungle.

"What is this?" Kristi gasped.

"No." Ty shook his head. "*When* is this?"

Arnold shouted from the bottom of the stairs. They sprinted through the hallways, out the front door, down the wide front steps. The campus looked like a scene from some cheesy end-of-the-world movie. The school's windows were all broken; the roof of the library caved in. Spray-painted plywood covered the doors and windows of the administration building. The trees were sickly, like poisoned skeletons with leafless, crooked fingers clawing at a somber gray sky. The air tasted tart and oily, like a freshly poured asphalt road.

"Look!" Kristi pointed above the front doors of the school. The sign, which once had spelled out *George Washington Prep* in big, blue letters, now read *B nedic Arn ld P ep*

"This is all wrong," Ty said, gripping his hair with both hands. "It's *Arnold's* world."

Just then, the man himself burst through the front doors, howling. "*Give me the time machine!*"

They sprinted up the hill to the soccer fields, now overgrown with grasses as tall as Kristi's chest. They pushed through, gasping, and ducked into the woods on the other side. After a few minutes of running, they jumped into a ditch and finally looked back. Kristi grimaced and held the stitch in her side. It now felt like a knife wound. She couldn't seem to pull in a full breath through the oily, acidic air, even in the middle of the woods.

"You s-see him?" she gasped.

"No. I think...he's gone," Ty said.

She exhaled and lay back, closing her eyes, clutching the time machine to her chest. "What's going on? What happened to our school?"

"I don't know, but we have to go back. In time, I mean. They're going to hang Stephen."

An even more terrible thought occurred then. So horrifying she almost threw up. "But Ty...they already did—two hundred years ago."

"No! I mean we can change it." He snatched the time machine and pushed a few buttons. No lights came on. "*Bleeding, bloody boogies*! It's *dead*. I think we have to charge it—find a-a computer or something."

"I'm not going back into that school!"

"Me neither. Not while Crazy Arnold is lurking about."

"If we can find a phone, I'll get my dad to pick us up."

"Your dad? I thought you hated the guy."

"Yeah. But he'd pound Arnold to a pulp if the creep touched us."

Ty hesitated. "Will he *believe* us?"

"He has to." She pointed to the time machine. "We have this. Besides, even *I* couldn't make up a story *this* crazy."

Ty nodded. "All right, let's go."

They made a wide circle, avoiding the school grounds, then left the woods and made their way up the gentle slope of a hill.

They stopped at the top and looked down. Nothing but long, empty fields. No roads. No houses. In the hazy distance, Kristi saw what looked like a wall stretching along the horizon. "What's that? Where's the city—the buildings—all the people? What in the world did Arnold *do*?"

Ty swallowed. "I don't know. Something really bad."

After a few miles, she spotted a house atop another hill. "Over there! Maybe there's a phone."

But as they got closer, she realized it wasn't a house. More a crumbling shack. Half the roof was missing. The dark squares in the walls held no windowpanes.

Ty stuck his head through the opening where a door should've been. "Hello—anyone home?" The pitiful place was empty, except for patchy weeds growing in a dirt floor.

"Guess we're walking," Kristi said.

Over the next few hours, they found nothing but overgrown fields and huge areas of cleared trees, just stumps left in the dusty ground. Finally, when Kristi was sure her legs couldn't carry her another step, she spotted a curl of pale smoke in the distance. They climbed the next slope and looked down. A village lay below, about twenty huts straggling along the bank of a small creek. At the far end, a gnarled, leafless oak stood between the last hut and the water.

"No," she whispered. "No, no, no. It's—it's all gone!"

Ty frowned. "What?"

She plopped on her rear and covered her face. "My house—it's—gone! It should be right there!" She pointed. "I had a tree house in that old oak. It was in my back yard. But everything's gone!"

Ty took her hand. "Come on. Your family—maybe they're in one of those, uh, houses."

They made their way down to a dirt lane leading into the village. Two children were playing outside the first hovel, one a dirty-face toddler in a ragged cloth diaper. The other was a boy with a filthy shirt and tattered, cut-off jeans who looked their own age. The toddler pointed at them and laughed, showing rotten teeth. Kristi waved. The boy glanced over and his eyes grew wide. He immediately scooped the toddler up and ran into a shack, yelling, "Momma, Momma!"

Kristi cringed. Ty squeezed her hand. They kept on past, walking faster. The rest of the shacks seemed empty. When they reached the oak, Kristi leaned back against it, slid down its trunk, wrapped her arms around her legs. "No, no," she moaned. "This can't be happening!"

A hunched black man stepped out of a nearby shack no bigger than her vanished tree house. When he noticed them, he froze. "Who are you?"

Kristi looked up. The man's face was a blur of dark skin through her tears. But as he tottered toward them, she pushed herself up, blinking the tears away. Her heart stuttered. "DAD!"

He stopped, eyes narrowing. "Who—"

"Daddy! It's me. *Kristi!*"

His frowned deepened. "You shouldn't be here, girl!" He grabbed her shirt, dragged her toward the shack.

"Hey! Get off her!" Ty yelled. He jumped on the man's back. The man threw him off, then dragged Kristi into the shack, and slammed its splintered door.

FOURTEEN

Kristi stood in one corner, across from the man she thought she knew as her father as Ty pounded on the door, shaking the unpainted clapboard walls of the shack.

The man leaned over the back of a chair, coughing as if he'd mistakenly inhaled water instead of air. Was it really Dad? He'd been so big and strong, like a linebacker. This man was tall, but hunched, bent by a hump twisting his shoulders, body emaciated. Thick lines creased the leather that was his face. Instead of her dad's familiar frizzy black hair, his was thin with more patches of skin showing than hair.

But his eyes, even though watery from coughing, were the same deep brown ones she'd stared into as a little girl.

"D—dad?" she said quietly.

He straightened a little, shook his head, but the hacking increased and he doubled again, looking like he'd keel over.

The door splintered, ripping from its flimsy tin hinges and Ty broke through, panting, haloed in dust. "Let her go!"

"Please—" the man choked, held up one finger. "Please—just—wait." His coughing calmed. He took a slow, raspy breath. "I don't mean her no harm."

"Don't you know who I am?" Kristi choked out.

He laughed, then started coughing again. Finally, he cleared his throat and spat on the dirt floor. "Ain't never seen you before in my life, girl."

Ty picked up a wooden chair and started toward him.

"No!" Kristi stepped in front of Ty. "Is your name James? James Connors?"

The man's face went ashen. Then he shook his head. "What if it is?"

She stepped to him, grabbed one hand. It was gnarled, knuckles swollen with arthritis. "Please. It's Kristi. Your *daughter!*"

He threw her hand off and backed into the corner she'd been in a moment earlier. "I ain't got no daughter."

She held a hand over her mouth. Her legs suddenly felt like thin, wobbly sticks.

Ty touched her shoulder. "Come on, Kristi. We're tired, hungry, out of sorts. You've got the wrong guy."

She knocked his hand off. "It *isn't* the wrong guy! I know my own dad!"

Connors sighed, shook his head. "Don't know what yer talkin' about, girl. Ain't got no kids. No wife, and no...reason to expect a surprise like you."

Kristi gripped her head with both hands. "What is *happening* to me?"

Connors edged sideways, toward the open doorway. "Where'd you all come from? Ain't been any other blacks walkin' free 'round here for twenty years or more."

"I'm *from* here," she snapped.

"Well, if the emperor's guards find the likes of you in my house, they'll know ya come through the Wall."

"*Wall?* What wall?" Ty said.

Connors stared, dumbstruck for a moment. "Why—THE Wall. No one gets past it without the emperor knowin'."

"What're you talking about?" Kristi cried. "Where are we?"

"Where ya think? Benedecia."

She dug her fingers into Ty's arm. "But—but what happened to Philadelphia?"

"Philla-what?" Connors shook his head. "Never heard of it."

"You're daft!" Ty raised the chair. "Get out of our way!"

"Well, go on then. But I'm tellin' you it ain't safe. The emperor's guards will shoot ya both."

"What emperor are you talking about?" Ty demanded.

The man gave an exasperated grunt. "Emperor *Arnold*. Who else?"

Kristi's breath caught. She dug her fingers harder. "You mean—*Xavier* Arnold?"

"Only Arnold left, ain't he? How 'bout you put that chair down and sit before your heads explode? *I* ain't gonna hurt nobody." Keeping his hands in sight, he scooted crab-wise to another wobbly wooden chair and sat.

Ty looked back at Kristi. She nodded, trying to look stronger than she felt. He set the chair down and put a hand on her shoulder. "Maybe he's wrong. I mean—"

Connors coughed and cleared his throat again. "Now, how'd you all get here?"

"We get answers first," Ty said. "Because—because it's an emergency. Tell us—how did Xavier Arnold become emperor?"

Connors shrugged. "How else. The way they always do it—killed his pa and took his place."

Kristi gasped. "He killed his own father?"

"Ah, he made it look like an accident, sure. But we all knowed better. They never did get along, always fightin' 'bout how to use us peasants. Labor force been dryin' up for years—" He coughed again, then smiled ruefully. "Been workin' in the mines since I turned twelve, see. We all have. It's where I got this here cough, jus' like everyone else."

Kristi shook her head. "But you're a lawyer, not a miner!"

"Ha!" Connors made a laughing sound, but his face was hard, unsmiling. "Ain't no lawyers in Benedicia, 'specially black 'uns. Only miners. But people got sick and stopped minin'. The empire was losin' lots of money. So Xavier, he wanted to use forced labor. The old emperor, he didn't. Next thing ya know, ol' Richard sorta *fell* down a coalmine shaft. Xavier got his forced labor decree, along with his pa's crown."

Kristi went rigid. "You mean, the workers are slaves, now."

Connors frowned, as if considering. "S'pose so. When Xavier took over, most the black people, *they* knowed what was comin'. Took off for the states. But I weren't quick enough."

"So there's still a place called the United States?" Ty asked.

"You been livin' under a rock? 'Course there is! People was leavin' for it in droves, black and white. So Xavier put up his Wall. Then no one could get in or out without him knowin'."

"I don't understand," Ty said. "Why isn't *this* the United States?"

Connors whistled. "You really have been under some rock. How far back you need me to go, boy?"

Ty ran his hand through his hair, glanced at Kristi. "All the way, I guess."

Connors straightened. "All right, then. Long time ago, we was all part of Britain. There was this big revolt. The first emperor, Benedict IV, helped squash it."

"Benedict *Arnold*?" Ty said.

"Yup. He hanged the rebel leaders so the British king made him Royal Governor. But the revolt also started a war with France. King couldn't afford to handle the colonies and fight a war, so he pulled the soldiers out and handed the place over to ol' Benedict."

"But how'd Benedict become *emperor*?"

"He raised an army and tried takin' it all. But nobody trusted him after what he done to the revolutionaries. After a bloody civil war, a treaty got signed and he got handed one of the biggest colonies. Named hisself emperor, called it Benedicia. Everything else became the United States of America. Over the years, Ben's offspring sold off bits and pieces to the American government. Now all that's left is the palace grounds and those blasted coal mines."

Kristi collapsed onto a chair. "What is *wrong* with the universe?"

"Couldn't tell you that," Connors said. "But you gotta get outta here while ya still can."

"We didn't come through the wall," Ty said. "We have a—a different way of traveling. We have to find a computer to— charge something."

Connors laughed. "You won't find none a' them contraptions, 'cept in the palace. But you ain't gettin' in there. No sir."

Kristi looked up. "Where is this palace?"

"Next to the river, surrounded by another wall. Guarded by a bunch of trigger-happy meatheads."

"Can you take us there?" Ty asked.

"You cracked, boy? I tol' ya. If they find ya, yer *toast.* Me too if they find out I helped ya."

Kristi sighed. "Arnold knows we're here."

"Then I already said too much!" Connors stood and made a hand-washing gesture. "Y'all hafta leave now."

"Please help us, Dad," she pleaded.

"Stop callin' me that, girl! Yer crazy talk is likely gonna get me killed. I don't need no more trouble." He herded them toward the door.

Kristi's chest squeezed as if in a vise. "Please!" she cried. "Your mom's name is Loretta. Your dad is James. You have two brothers and a sister."

Connors stopped, took a step back. "Don' try no Gypsy voodoo on me, girl."

"Please, just listen to us."

"We need your help, sir," Ty said. "We *have* to get into the palace."

Connors laughed and shook his head. "Yer both two bricks short of a load. It's too dangerous."

"We don't have a choice," Ty said. "And besides, we can— change things for everyone—if we do."

"Please, Da—I mean, Mr. Connors." She approached carefully, took his hands again. He flinched, but let her hold them in hers. "Wouldn't you like to see things get better? Don't you want this terrible emperor put down?"

He cocked his head to the side and looked into her eyes, then snorted. "'Course I do! Killed a lot o' my buddies. Jus' don' see how a couple cracked kids can do anythin' 'bout it."

Kristi nodded to Ty. He pulled the time-travel rod from his jacket. "It's—well—a sort of time machine. Xavier Arnold invented it so he could go back into the past. He changed history, and made himself emperor."

Connors's forehead wrinkled. "Say what?"

Ty sighed. "I know it's hard to believe, but—"

145

"Well I'll be." Connors fell back, had another coughing fit and spat in the dirt again. "So it's true!"

Kristi and Ty exchanged confused glances. "You mean—you believe us?" she said.

"E'erybody knows 'bout the emperor's wild experiments. People used to say he was tryin' to build a time travel contraption—but I never believed a word of it."

"It's all true," Ty said. "Only, it wasn't supposed to end up like this. This should *all* be America, with houses and schools and airports. Xavier changed everything, for the worse."

Connors squinted at him. "So what can you two squits do 'bout it?"

"Go back and set things right. But we need to get to a computer. Please, you *have* to help us."

Kristi squeezed his hands. "I know this all sounds crazy. But you *were* my father in a different, better world. Arnold took that away from me—from us. We can get it back."

Tears welled in Connors' eyes. He opened his mouth to say something, but his lips trembled. He finally grunted, stepped over to the small, grimy window and stared out. "Lord he'p me. *I* must be cracked." He scratched his head and sighed. "Okay, then. I'll get you over to the palace. Show you a way in. But get caught and ye'll be on yer own. Don't say a word 'bout me."

Ty laid a hand over his heart. Kristi did likewise. "You have our solemn promise on that."

***

When Kristi was small, her mother had read her countless fairytales of palaces with golden thrones, of fairy godmothers, handsome knights, and kindly kings.

But Arnold's palace looked like a maximum-security prison, not a fantasy castle. The buildings were boxy gray concrete, windowless, surrounded by a twenty-foot wall with men atop it carrying rifles. A giant brick smokestack towered from the center of the compound, blanketing the sky with smoke. *No wonder the air tastes so bad*, she thought.

Connors had given them some food and water, then left them at the edge of the woods. They'd hiked until the top of the wall was in view, then, staying hidden in the trees, worked their way around the compound until they came to the dirt lane in back. Metal warehouse-type doors in the great wall stood at the end, guarded by a lone man with a rifle and a clipboard, who paced back and forth.

So they'd climbed the hill and hunkered behind some bushes on a rise overlooking the compound, waiting.

Now Kristi's stomach growled. She fingered the apple in her pocket, but her stomach felt too wrenched to eat. She wasn't even supposed to be *alive* in this world.

"What are we going to do?" she asked, shaking that last thought from her head.

"Find a way to sneak in that door, I guess."

An engine sputtered from over the hill. A rusty yellow dump truck lurched into view and trundled past, its bed filled with glistening black chunks of coal. A train of wagons straggled behind, pulled by horses and mules. The drivers' faces and clothes were black with coal dust.

The truck stopped at the metal doors, idling while the guard circled it and made notes on his clipboard. The doors creaked open slowly. The truck coughed and backfired, then sputtered into the compound, reappearing minutes later with an empty bed, and left by a different road.

The guard inspected each load, each wagon, before letting it pass.

Ty shook his head. "So much for the sneaking-in scheme."

After nearly an hour, the last wagon entered and exited. But the doors stayed open. The guard flipped through the papers on his clipboard, then scowled up the hill, as if waiting for something—something that was very late.

"Now what?" said Kristi.

Ty rubbed his chin. "I don't know. Maybe we—"

Distant cursing interrupted him. Another wagon rocked slowly over the hill, pulled by a skinny white mule that seemed to be out for a Sunday stroll. The driver snapped the reins and swore again, but the swaybacked creature ignored him,

147

stopping every few steps to tear up mouthfuls of grass from the side of the road.

"*Yer* gonna be dinner tonight if I don't make my delivery!" the driver howled.

"Give me your apple," Ty said. "I have an idea."

She handed it over. He ran down the slope toward the wagon. She pulled her hood up and followed, staying close behind him—though, with all the coal dust, the driver's face looked blacker than hers.

Ty grabbed the mule's bridle. "Need a hand, sir?"

"Git your paws off my mule, boy!"

Ty ignored him and rubbed the animal's neck. "How about a snack, girl?" He held out the apple. The mule perked up and snapped at it. He pulled back, holding the fruit a foot away. As the beast lurched forward, Ty backed down the road, leading her along in spurts of apple-lust.

The driver frowned. "Don't be expectin' me to pay you nothin', boy."

"Maybe just a meal for me and—and my sister?"

Kristi almost laughed at the piteous look Ty gave the man.

The driver threw his hands up and sat back. "Fine! Just get me there afore them doors close, and I'll feed ya both. But that's all."

They worked their way down the road, one on either side of the mule. Kristi rubbed its head. "Just a little further, girl."

As they approached the doors, she ducked behind the wagon. The guard stepped out and scowled. "You're late, Homer!"

"Sorry," the driver muttered. "Trouble with this durned cat-meat critter again."

"Not my problem. It's gonna cost ya."

"I got enough to cover it."

The guard glanced at Ty and his scowl deepened. "These river rats belong to you?"

Kristi ducked her head.

"Just a couple kids helpin' out," the driver wheedled. "Please, Johns. It's almost curfew."

The guard huffed and flipped the pages on his clipboard. "Get unloaded, then. If I'm late for dinner, I'll fine you double tomorrow."

The driver snapped the reins and Ty lured the mule on through the doors.

Inside, the warehouse looked like an airplane hangar with a concrete floor, high ceiling, and tall dirty windows to let in light. The air hung heavy with dust from the mountain of coal that sat in the middle of the floor.

"I'll throw in breakfast if you get me unloaded fast," the driver told them.

Ty nodded. Kristi spotted a line of men on the other side of the coal pile, all loading wheelbarrows in turn, then pushing them up a ramp and through a door. When one disappeared with a full barrow, another appeared with an empty one. *That* was their way in. She pointed, and Ty nodded.

They took turns trundling wheelbarrows up behind the wagon while the man shoveled black lumps into them, then wheeled the barrows over and dumped them on the pile. When the wagon was almost empty, the driver turned his back on them, kicked the remaining bits of coal off the back of the wagon.

They took this chance to duck away and hide on the other side of the big pile. There, Ty rubbed a lump of coal between his hands, then blackened his face and clothes with the dust. Then they joined the line moving up a long ramp to a corridor lit by flickering yellow bulbs. It was just wide enough to for their wheelbarrows to graze the empty ones going back. The men pushing them all looked the same: cropped hair, filthy clothes, blackened, work-worn faces. None even glanced up as they passed.

After turning a few corners and climbing another long ramp, they followed the line through a door. A wave of heat blasted out, taking their breath. A giant furnace was smoking against a far wall, its ten-foot, fiery maw a hungry dragon's mouth. Two men with huge shovels were sweating to keep it fed.

The man in front of them dumped his load onto a smaller pile, then left.

"Now's our chance," Ty whispered.

They left the wheelbarrows, turned down another corridor. This one was narrower, the floor also concrete. They passed a handful of doors, trying the handles of each. Two opened, but only led to closets full of mops, buckets, and brooms.

A stairwell stood at the end of the hall. As they got closer, Kristi felt a breeze.

"Up or down?" Ty asked.

Both sets of stairs turned after ten steps. The landings were dark. Kristi held out her hand. The breeze was coming from above. "Up."

So they climbed. The next level looked just like hallway they'd left, concrete floor and dim, flickering lights. The breeze coming down the stairs was stronger, though. A low hum vibrated the steps beneath their feet. They kept climbing and came upon two fans on the next level, blowing down the stairwell. Past these was a brighter hallway with clean blue carpeting. The air was sweeter, clear of dust.

"If you were a computer, where would you be?" Ty said.

She smiled wistfully. "In a coffee shop with a double, decaf mocha latte with whipped cream and cinnamon sprinkles."

Ty grinned. "All right, then. Let's find the barista." He tried the first door, which opened. He poked his head in. "Check this room. I'll try the next. Give a whistle if you see anything useful."

Instead of a Starbucks, Kristi found a small office, its gray desk covered with papers and notebooks. Also a metal cabinet and a bookshelf packed with books. No computer, though. She rooted through drawers, looking for a laptop, but only discovered more binders. The cabinet doors were locked, but she found a set of keys in the middle desk drawer. Manila files and black binders packed its shelves. Just as she started to close its doors, a dim, blue light caught her eye. She moved a stack of notebooks and her heart jumped. A *laptop*! She tried to whistle for Ty, but her lips were so dry she only blew soundlessly. Heart pattering like a crazed drummer, she opened the computer. The screen flashed blue.

She slammed the lid and turned to go get Ty. As she did, the bookcase scraped back like a door. She was suddenly face to stomach with the largest man she'd ever seen. His big, shaved head dwarfed hers. His black shirt stretched to contain muscles even bigger than her head.

His forehead wrinkled, eyes widening. A knowing smile spread his lips. "Ah ha! We all been looking for you, girl."

She threw the computer at him. He swatted it away like a scrap of paper and clamped onto her arm. "Not so fast, sweety. You got yourself a date. With the emperor himself."

She kicked his shins, but he picked her up easily. When she screamed and swung at his face, he only laughed, then heaved her up onto one shoulder. She squirmed and beat on his back, flailing, knocking papers and binders from the desk. It made no difference. The ogre carried her away behind the bookcase into a grim darkness.

FIFTEEN

Ty tore down the hall and burst into the room where he'd left Kristi. But she was gone. The blizzard of papers across the desktop and the broken laptop on the floor showed there'd been a struggle.

"Kristi!" He swung the cabinet doors open, dropped and looked under the desk.

Then a muffled yell filtered through the bookcase. He jumped up, leaned an ear against a row of spines, heard faint scuffling on the other side. He ripped all the books down, but the back of the case was solid oak.

Another cry came through, fainter this time. He banged on the wood and got back a hollow echo. When he pushed, the case gave an inch. Leaning into it, he drove hard until a gap between wall and bookcase opened, then squeezed into a dark passageway.

Somewhere ahead, Kristi was shouting, "Put me down, you big jerk!"

He followed her voice, sliding one hand over a damp rock wall. After a while, he tripped, banged his knee on something—a step. He grimaced, thankful the unseen stairs led up instead of down. A faint white light flickered at the top. He crawled up, stopping at the last riser to peer over.

The stairwell led to a large chamber with stone-gray walls and dozens of tables holding blue-screened computers. In the middle of the room three steps led to a platform where more computers sat beneath a wall-sized flat screen, divided into six smaller screens. The room with the huge coal pile appeared on one. The furnace on another. Various corridors were monitored on the rest.

Ty gritted his teeth. Arnold could've been watching them the whole time they'd been in the complex.

A huge man, who resembled a forest giant in a fairy tale, stood just before the steps, holding Kristi at arm's length as she kicked and punched at him. He was easily seven feet tall with tree trunk legs and big, beefy arms. Ty waited for the giant to turn his back, then slid under the nearest table and started yanking on computer cords.

A metal door under the flat-screen scraped open. Dr. Arnold strolled in. His filthy colonial shirt and torn leather breeches were gone. In their place he wore knee pants of golden cloth and a white silk shirt. A long velvet maroon robe edged with gold fringe swept the floor behind him. "What do we have here?"

The giant bowed, still gripping Kristi. "Caught her snoopin' in an office, Yer Eminence."

Arnold laughed. "Not the smartest girl on the block, are you?" He nodded to the giant, who dropped her. "What do you think of my new world, Ms. Connors?"

Kristi shook her head, chuckled. "Which part—the dirty air, the crumbling shacks, the slaves who want to kill you? It fits you."

"Ahh, from the mouths of babes." Arnold's eyes twinkled. "I admit this wasn't exactly what I had in mind. But I'm *emperor*. Who better to bring Benedicia to prominence?"

Ty kept pulling cords. Three came loose, dangled down. The connectors of the first two were too small to fit the time-rod, but the third slid right into the machine. The blue and red lights flashed dimly along its length. He held it to his chest to cover the glow.

Arnold bent to poke a finger in Kristi's face. "Where's our little British matey, and my favorite toy? Can't rewrite history without it." He winked.

She tried to bite his hand, but he jerked it out of reach. "He's long gone."

"You lie badly."

"He went back in time with your stupid machine to find George Washington and tell him all about Benedict Arnold. You're never even gonna be born, now."

Arnold tsked. "That's not what a little birdy told me."

The sound of a hacking cough came through the still open door. Two guards stepped in, dragging the limp body of a black man between them. He had a gash across the top of his patchy bald head. His bottom lip was split, dripping blood. One eye was swollen shut, the other wide and horror-stricken.

"Daddy!" Kristi cried.

"I'm sorry," Connors wheezed.

"Daddy?" Arnold glanced back and forth between them, then grinned. "My, hasn't this become interesting."

Ty gritted his teeth and started punching buttons on the rod. A screen the size of a business card flashed green. *Tarrytown: New York: 23 September, 1780: 9:32 AM.* The exact moment they'd left. But if he went back to that exact time, it would still be too late. André would have already gotten through the crossroads. He pushed it back twelve hours. That should give them enough time.

The lights on the machine dimmed for a horrifying second. "Come *on*," he groaned. Then they brightened and rolled up and down the length of the rod, like a crowd doing the wave at a football match.

"Tell me where the boy is and we won't have to hurt your *daddy* anymore," Arnold said to Kristi.

"Don't!" Connors blurted. One guard backhanded him and he slumped. They let go and he slid to the floor in a heap.

"Stop!" Kristi shouted.

Arnold raised his eyebrows. "Give me a reason to."

She crossed her arms and scowled. "Fine. I'll tell *if* you let us go. My dad, too."

"Of course." Arnold shrugged, showed his palms. "I certainly don't *want* to hurt you."

Kristi crossed her arms. "Ty's hiding in the bushes by the road at the top of the hill."

Arnold turned to the guards over Connors. "Find the boy and get the machine!"

They hesitated, looked down at Connors' still form.

"He's not going anywhere. Get my *machine!*"

"And the boy, your grace?" the other asked.

Arnold winked at Kristi. "Oh, I don't think we need him anymore."

"You said you wouldn't hurt us!" Kristi yelled.

Arnold yawned. "Oh, an *emperor* can't be held to remember precisely what he says from one moment to the next."

She lunged at him, but the giant caught her and threw her down again.

The guards left. Connors stirred, lifted his head, and looked around in confusion. Ty waved, caught his attention. The miner's good eye blinked, then widened. Ty held up a finger for silence and the man nodded slightly.

Ty pushed ENTER. The lights sped up. He flashed a thumbs-up.

Connors struggled to his feet. "I got somethin' to say, Yer Highness."

"Sorry, old man. Peasants in *my* empire aren't given a say."

Connors glared. "I'll have my say if it kills me."

Arnold raised one eyebrow. "It may."

James Connors, Kristi's dad in another world, leaned his head back and spat blood toward Arnold. "You're no emperor. Not mine. Not anymore. You jus' a bully who likes pickin' on kids."

Arnold yawned again. "Shut him up, please."

The giant cracked his knuckles, stepped over Kristi. Connors only lifted his chin and stood straight, looking more defiant than afraid.

Ty crawled out and bent the time machine into a halo. When the wind tunnel roared from its center, the heating metal ring almost flew from his hands. His knuckles grew white with strain as the ceiling lights surged and popped like firecrackers, dropping darkness on them like a stage curtain. The halo flashed *blueredblueredbluered*.

Arnold's jaw dropped. *"You!"* He stepped toward Ty, but Kristi jumped up, rammed her head into his stomach. When he gasped and doubled, she pulled his robe over his head.

"Not the smartest emperor on the block, are you?" she said, then ran to Ty and wrapped her arms around his waist.

The giant man turned from Connors, lumbered toward them. Just before his meaty hands could grasp them, Ty dropped the halo onto Kristi's head. They shot off into the sickening swirl of lights, screaming.

***

Ty came to, face down in the dirt. His ears picked up the buzz of crickets, the hoot of an owl. He turned over and saw trees above him, dusk settling in the sky.

He groaned and held his head. "There's got to be a better way to time travel."

"Tell me about it," Kristi grumbled. She looked around and her eyes widened. "Oh no—My dad! What're they going to do to him?"

"Nothing, if we can stop Dr. Arnold. If I did this right, it should be the night before Arnold's men ambush the crossroads. We have to get to the jail and break Stephen and our, uh, *other* selves out."

Kristi gaped. "Our *other* selves? What the heck are you talking about?"

"I brought us back twelve hours *before* the attack in the woods. Before we went forward in time with Arnold. I think our other selves will still be here, locked in the jail."

"There are *two* of us, now?"

"Exactly."

"So how do we get them—or us, or whatever they are—out?"

He grinned. "I have a smashing scheme. Perfect for your talents."

***

It was fully dark by the time they reached Tarrytown. They'd hid across the street from the jailhouse, waited another hour for Arnold to leave for the inn. The skinny constable had been with him, leaving only the fat one behind.

Now Kristi stood in front of the door. She took a deep breath, then stepped inside. Hog-Face was snoring in a chair, feet up on the desktop. "Hey, Sheriff Fatty."

He jerked awake and his chair crashed over, shaking the jailhouse. He cursed and pushed himself up again, rubbing one elbow. "Blazes! How'd you get out?"

"What, from that chintzy cell?" She snapped her fingers. "Easy as apple pie."

"I'll give ya apple pie!" he roared, rolling to his feet.

She ran back out the door. When he stepped across the threshold, Ty hit him over the head with a thick branch, knocked him to the ground, where he lay still.

Kristi let out a long breath. "Hey! Not bad, limey."

"Thanks." He grabbed one meaty arm. "Come on, help me out here." They heaved the massive body back inside, then closed the door.

She grabbed the keys off the jailer's belt and grinned. "Can't wait to see the looks on our own faces when we see us."

Ty chuckled. "There are *so* many things wrong with that sentence."

He took a lantern and they descended the stone steps. In the basement, Stephen and the other Ty sat against the far wall. The other Kristi lay curled on the floor, eyes closed.

Kristi clanked the keys along the iron. "Wake up, sleepy heads! Up and at 'em."

The jailed Ty looked up, stared for a confused second, then rubbed his eyes. "*What in the bloody—*"

She laughed. "Hi! Ready to get outta there?"

The jailed Ty stared for another second, then shook the other Kristi.

"What?" she mumbled. "Leave me alone."

"Uh...Kristi. You're gonna want to...see this."

She opened her eyes, stared, then scrambled back. "What—how—oh my—*what's going on?*"

"Come on," the free Ty said. "We'll explain later."

Kristi unlocked the cell and the other Kristi stepped tentatively out. They looked each other up and down. "Man, I look horrible!" they said in unison, then both laughed uncertainly.

"Where'd you two come from?" Stephen said.

Kristi grinned. "The future. Where else?"

"But how?"

"Dr. Arnold's plan worked," Ty said as they climbed the stairs. "André got through. Then British captured George Washington at West Point. Benedict Arnold got all the credit. In the new future, Dr. Arnold's the *emperor of Benedicia*—what used to be Pennsylvania."

"What?" The other Kristi gasped. "How can *that* be? *Emperor?*"

"It's a long, bad story," he said and held up the time machine. "We stole this one from Arnold and came back to fix it. But the Arnold *in this time* still has one, too. We have to get him before he stops André's capture again." He turned to Stephen. "We have about nine hours before Arnold and his men ambush the militiamen at the crossroads. I need you to take these two and find help." He pointed to the other Kristi and Ty, then handed the time machine to the other Ty. "If something goes wrong, there should be enough juice left to get you out of here."

Stephen frowned. "Then you've got no machine. How are you going to get back?"

Ty tapped a keg of gunpowder sitting on the counter. "We're gonna nick Arnold's."

***

Kristi led the way to the crossroads with the torch while Ty lugged the keg at a safe distance from the flame. After what felt like hours stumbling through the dark, they found a clearing overlooking the road and hunkered down, waited for daylight. They took turns sleeping against a tree and keeping watch.

Now a thin mist covered the hill in the grey half-light of morning. Songbirds filled the trees. Bleary-eyed, Kristi watched as Ty backed through the trees, pouring a thin trail of black, grainy powder over the ground. He brought a long fuse back to their hiding spot, then poured a wide pile connecting the trail to the three he'd already laid. He rolled the empty keg into a nearby bush.

"Tell me the plan again," she said. "I mean, the *scheme.*"

"Remember, Arnold will be hiding there." He pointed to the boulders twenty yards down the hill. "His men will be positioned there, there, there, and there, like before." He pointed to four trees spread out across the hill. "If Stephen and our other selves don't get here in time, we'll light the gunpowder and hope the blasts drive them away." He laid flint and steel next to the trailhead.

"What if the wind blows some of it away?"

"Then I guess we'd be buggered."

"Well, *great!* How much time—"

"Shhh," Ty said. "Look."

Dr. Arnold and four men with muskets over their shoulders came marching and stopped at the crossroad. Kristi and Ty ducked behind a rosebay bush and peered through its spiny leaves. Arnold pointed up the hill. The men climbed the slope and fanned out, the four going right to the places Ty had pointed out, Arnold to his boulders.

Kristi's heart thumped like a bongo. She squeezed Ty's arm. "Stephen's not going to get here in time."

"Maybe not." He picked up the flint and steel. "I'm ready, just in case."

They waited. Finally, the militiamen arrived on the road. At Arnold's whistle, his men stood and fired, sending clouds of white smoke rising through the trees. Musket balls peppered the dirt at the militiamen's feet. They moved to the trees on either side of the road and fired back.

"Here goes." Ty kissed the flint, then scraped it against steel. A shower of golden sparks rained on the powder. It popped and sputtered for a second, then a spiral of acrid smoke rose. Sizzling streams of fire shot along the trails in four directions.

"Wow," said Kristi. "Cool!" It was just like the Wile E. Coyote cartoons she used to watch with her dad.

Fireballs and black smoke erupted at the feet of Arnold's men. When the breeches of one caught fire, he screamed and rolled on the ground. The others jumped back, cursing. The militiamen heeded the lull and regained the road, forming a line across its breadth.

"NOW!" Ty yelled.

The two of them rushed Arnold. Kristi got there first and head-butted the teacher back into the boulder. This time, she ducked under his elbow as he swung back at her. Ty got him in a headlock and they all went down in a heap.

"Help!" Arnold yelled, but she clapped a hand over his mouth.

The ambushers regrouped, moved down the hill to new positions and fired. The militiamen scattered, opening the road again.

André appeared on the same brown horse, galloping toward the crossing, just as before.

"He's going to get through!" Kristi yelled. "Somebody stop him!"

Just before he reached the crossroads, another string of musket fire cracked the air. André's horse braced its legs and stopped, almost throwing André over its head. He regained his seat, though, reined the horse around, and sped back the way he'd come.

A dozen men in blue coats streamed onto the road. Two on horseback rode André down, pulling him out of the saddle. The others aimed up the hill and fired. Now outnumbered, Arnold's men scattered like spooked deer.

"They got him!" Kristi cried, hugging Ty.

Arnold took advantage of that moment to buck them off, knocking Ty's head into the boulder, tossing Kristi into a holly bush. He scrambled to his feet and stumbled up the hill.

Kristi pulled herself out of the bush, wincing at the cuts and scratches from the spiny leaves. She helped Ty up. He staggered, a hand on the back of his head.

"You okay?" she said, putting an arm around his waist to steady him.

"Yeah. I think so." He blinked and shook his head. "Come on."

They followed Arnold's path up the hill, pushing through bushes, ducking under low branches. The canopy thickened and the forest dimmed.

"Where'd he go?" Kristi panted.

A shout ripped through the trees ahead. They broke into a run. When they rounded an oak as wide as a park bench, there was Arnold, arm wrapped around the other Kristi's neck. The other Ty faced him, gripping a branch like a club. The teacher spun the other Kristi, keeping her between himself and the weapon.

"Let her go!" Kristi yelled.

Arnold looked up and his eyes widened. "Wh—who the heck are *you*?"

The three of them surrounded Arnold. She and Ty picked up branches too. They slowly closed in.

"Back off!" Arnold squeezed the other Kristi's neck until her face turned red and she gasped for breath.

They stopped in their tracks. "Just let her go!" Kristi yelled. "It's over!"

"Over?" Arnold's face twisted with incredulity. He laughed. "*You* don't tell *me* when it's over, girl. *I have all the time in the world!*"

His free hand grabbed the other time machine from under his coat. He held it against his hip and bent it into a halo. Lights flashed and wind roared, pushing them further back. "Wonder how she'll like Ancient Egypt," he yelled over the noise, eyes gleaming, reflecting the sparkle of blue and red lights. He started to lower the halo, but the other Kristi ducked, bit his wrist, and stomped his foot. He howled and she broke away, stumbling into the other Ty's arms.

Arnold raised the halo to crown his own head. Just before it touched his brow, orange fire erupted in a bush behind him. A loud bang sounded even over the roaring cyclone of the time-wind. A musket ball ripped into Arnold's thigh. He squealed, dropping the machine into the leaves. Ty rushed forward, swung the branch like a bat and hit the teacher in the gut with a loud *thwap*. Arnold crumpled to the ground. The other Ty grabbed the halo and pulled it apart. The wind slowed, the leaves stilled. The woods were suddenly quiet.

A tall silhouette emerged from the trees.

"Stephen!" Kristi cried.

The old farmer, once a physicist in another life, stepped up to stand over the body of his former teacher, the musket in his hands still smoking. "Time's up, Xavier," he said.

SIXTEEN

ay goodbye to **Martha** for me." Kristi hugged Stephen. "Tell her not to worry about me filling my family's shoes. There isn't a pair in the world big enough to hold me back."

"Hug her for both of us," the other Kristi said.

Stephen smiled. "Will do."

Kristi glanced at her twin, then at both Tys, who stood to the side, like mirrored images. They looked hesitant, nervous. "This is *so* weird," she said. "I still don't get what's going to happen next. Are there still going to be two sets of us when we get back to our time? That's going to be pretty tough to explain."

Her twin grinned. "But that'd mean half the homework, half the chores."

Kristi considered this a moment. "Huh-uh. I'm a few hours older, remember? You could change your name. How about Chevette?"

The other girl snorted. "Maybe if I was a rusty old car. I'll just go with Kristine. What about you two?" She looked at the Tys. "Can we call one of you Rufus? Or how about Alistair?"

Ty wrinkled his nose. "I don't think so."

"Just plain Thomas," said the other. "It's our middle name."

Stephen put a hand on the boys' shoulders. "I don't think it will matter. There are two sets now only because two of you went forward to a changed world, and came back again a little

163

earlier. The proper future should be restored, now. If so, nobody's coming back this time. My guess is you'll merge inside the portal."

"Too bad," Kristine said. "Thanksgiving dinner would've been a *blast!*"

"What's going to happen to Dr. Arnold?" Ty asked.

"Since he wanted to make history so badly, we'll let him stay here and be part of it," Stephen said. "I'm sure they'll find him a comfortable prison ship off shore."

"That's too good for the likes of him," Thomas said, scowling.

"So." Kristi turned to Ty. "You ready to go back?"

He and his other self glanced at each other. Thomas nodded and nudged him forward. Ty took a deep breath. "Actually...we're—uh—not going back."

"What?" Kristi and Kristine said in unison.

"We're staying here, with Stephen," Thomas added. "There's nothing back there for us. No family or friends. Just our jerk of a step-dad who couldn't stand one of us, let alone two."

Kristi's throat tightened. "But *I'm* your friend. I mean—we both are."

Thomas took Kristine's hands and Ty took Kristi's. "Please try to understand," Ty said. "We're better off here, in a world where we're needed and wanted. Stephen can't run the farm alone. We can help him."

Kristi's chest felt like a giant python was squeezing it. She looked down. Somehow, deep down, she'd already known. She'd seen how happy Ty had been on the farm, how comfortable he'd been in this time. It made sense, actually. This seemed to be where he belonged. Both of them. But understanding didn't make it any easier.

"Well then...I'm going to miss you, Froggy." Two tears dripped off her nose.

"Me too, Rich-Girl. You better become a powerful lawyer someday, after all the time and trouble I've gone to for you."

"Ha!" She grinned. "Maybe I will—between soccer seasons." She tapped the machine hanging off his hip. "You're keeping that one, right? There's still a little juice left in it. Might change your mind someday."

He winked. "Maybe."

She looked at Kristine. "You staying, too?"

"Sorry, girlfriend. You're stuck with me—or am I stuck with you?"

"I guess we'll find out." She hugged Ty again. "Be safe, limey. Be happy."

"I'll never forget you, Kristi." He smiled. "Send my regards to Dr. Marks. And that fat wanker Jeffrey."

She punched her hand and smirked. "With pleasure." She stepped back and took Kristine's hand. They each bent one end of the time machine until it formed a circle. Kristi mouthed *Thank you* through the roaring wind, then lowered the machine onto Kristine's head.

The two girls hurtled forward, mouths agape in screams. Time spun like a merry-go-round with rocket boosters, until Kristi's stomach felt like it was turning inside out. She squeezed Kristine's hand, fought to keep her eyes on her twin, to see what would happen in the portal. But the pressure in her head felt like she was at the bottom of a fifty-foot swimming pool. Finally, she had to close her eyes, afraid they'd simply pop out like marbles and spin away.

Then came a jolt, like a punch to her chest. Kristine's hand was gone, leaving Kristi grasping only air. The pressure intensified, and she passed out.

When she awoke, she felt a hard floor beneath her, but the wicked merry-go-round kept going around and around. She groaned and cradled her head, swallowing, trying not to get sick. Finally the spinning stopped. When she dared to open her eyes, she saw the underside of a rusted card table. She crawled out and looked around. Burned-out laptops with smoke rising from the keyboards sat on top of that card table and the one next to it. A single bulb hanging from the ceiling flickered. The rest were shattered. The flat-screen on the wall was a spidery pane of broken glass, like someone had thrown a baseball through it.

"Kristine!" She called and searched the lab and office. "Hello?" But no one else was there. Kristine was gone, or perhaps part of her again. There was no Ty or Thomas, either.

She sighed, then climbed onto the table and reached up to hide the time machine atop one of the bare rafters. She jumped down and took the stairs up to the main level of the school two at a time. Pausing at the top, she was suddenly unable to catch her breath. What if Arnold's terrible world hadn't changed? What if the school was still destroyed? What if her dad still didn't know her? She couldn't fix all that, not by herself.

Finally, she managed to pull in a lungful of air, then steeled herself for whatever was to come. Ty was gone, but she could still feel him with her. She felt Kristine, too, giving her strength. She took another deep breath and pushed through the door.

The hallway was a seething mass of khakis and red polos as uniformed kids rushed between classes. The lockers were painted bright blue, the speckled linoleum floor shiny with wax. *George Washington Prep* hung on the wall in big, white letters.

The hallway suddenly fell silent. Kristi was aware of gawking eyes, dropped jaws. Everyone was staring. She looked down. Her feet were bare and dirty, her legs scratched. Her old-fashioned shift was shredded, soiled, as if she'd wrestled a crocodile, then slept in a pigpen. She raised a hand. Her hair felt like a tangled bird's nest.

"Look out, it's swamp thing!" Jeffrey pushed through the crowd, smirking henchmen at each shoulder. "What happened? Did Froggy take you swimming in his scummy pond?"

It was too much, after all that'd happened. After all they'd done to fix this stupid jerk's world.

"His name is TY!" She cocked a fist and punched Jeffrey in the nose. The ring of students that had surrounded them gasped. The bully fell back into the lockers with a clang of fat on metal. The henchmen stood frozen, mouths agape. They tried to step back, but were stopped by the encircling crowd. Their eyes widened like mice cornered by a hungry cat.

"Right. Who's next?" Kristi yelled and shook a fist. The henchmen squeaked and scattered.

Kristi let them go. She stepped over Jeffrey. His nose was bleeding, eyes streaming tears. He trembled like a Chihuahua in a thunderstorm. She nudged one leg and he curled into a ball. "Don't hurt me!"

"Oh for—get out of here before I give you something to cry about, you whiny baboon."

He scrambled onto hands and knees, tried crawling away. Kristi couldn't resist. She pulled back and kicked him a good one right in the rear. He squealed like a piglet and skittered down the hall on all fours.

Every mouth in the crowd hung open, faces wavering between fear and awe. She suddenly felt self-conscious and tried to smooth her hair, to wipe the dirt off her face with one sleeve.

Then—someone clapped. A few others joined in. Soon everyone was applauding, laughing, patting her back. Almost as if she'd freed them from some bloodthirsty tyrant.

"What's going on here?" The elderly janitor pushed into the crowd, his wrinkled face scowling. "Break it up! Get to class!"

She ducked into the stream of students and let the flow carry her away. She left the school, crossed the quad, and headed for the administration building.

When she pushed into the offices, the secretary wrinkled her nose. "Oh my goodness. Can I help you, uh—"

"Here to see Dr. Marks."

"I'm sorry, miss, uh—but he's busy. If you could leave a—a note, I'll see he gets it."

"That's okay, Ms. Cunningham. He won't mind if I go right on in." She rounded the desk and pushed open the door to the dean's office.

"Get back here, young lady!" the secretary screeched.

"Hi, Dr. Marks!" Kristi called.

The dean was sitting behind his desk, leaning over a ledger. When he looked up, the color drained from his face. His hand clenched, snapping his pencil in half.

The secretary grabbed her arm. "I'm sorry, sir. I told this—this young lady—that you were busy."

"It's okay, Mildred." Dr. Marks pushed back his chair and stood. His hands trembled as he buttoned his suit jacket.

Ms. Cunningham scowled at her, then left. Kristi sat, propped her dirty bare feet on the desk, and leaned back with hands clasped behind her head. "Miss me, Marky?"

"Hardly. Where's Dr. Arnold?"

"Oh—he says hi. I think he's floating out on a prison ship somewhere. Maybe he'll send you a postcard from 1780."

He narrowed his eyes. "I see. But how did you—"

"You've got much bigger things to worry about than me. Like how fast you're going to leave this school and never, ever come back."

"You can't tell me what to do, you little fool!" A vein in his temple throbbed. "I'm the dean of—"

"The dean of *nothing*, now. You're outta here."

"Or what? Are you going to *tell on me*?" He pushed out his lip and wiped a fake tear from his cheek. "You, the spoiled brat who's done nothing but cause trouble all year. Think dear ol' Daddy will believe a word you say?"

She shook her head. "Oh, no, Dr. Marks. I'd never tell on you. You're right. Everyone would just think I'm crazy."

"That's right." The dean smirked, leaned against his desk. "Now run along like a good little girl."

Kristi scratched her head, as if contemplating, then shook it and stood. "Nah. Instead, how about I take *my* time machine back to find you when you were ten years old." She punched her palm. "We could have some real fun then, don't you think?" She turned toward the door.

"Wait! *Your* time machine?" His face turned whiter than the papers on his desk. "What're you talking about?"

Her turn to smirk. "Payback, Marky. You sent me to 1780 to be sold as a slave, remember? I owe you a good turn, too."

He clasped his hands but the fingers still twitched. "That was all Arnold's fault. I didn't want to—"

She lifted one muddy wrist, glanced at it as if she wore a watch. "Uh-oh. Time's running out. What if I go back just a little further, make sure you're never even born." She reached for the doorknob, then looked back and winked. "I'll see you real soon."

"Okay, okay. I'll leave." He started stuffing papers into a briefcase.

She raised her eyebrows. "A little faster, please."

"Please," he sputtered. "I can't just—"

"Oops. Time's up!"

He gasped and rushed past her, out of the office.

"Wanker." She chuckled. She went around the desk, sat in his big leather chair and spun it. Then picked up the phone. All the strength suddenly left her. The receiver shook in her hand as she punched in the familiar numbers, then listened to the ringing at the other end.

"Hello?"

"Daddy! You're okay!"

"Kristi. What's wrong? Why are you calling in the middle of the day?"

She let out a long breath, relieved that he knew who she was. She steadied her voice. "Nothing's wrong, Daddy. I just wanted to hear your voice."

He gave a heavy sigh. "Are you in trouble again?"

She bit back an angry retort. After all, he had no idea how much trouble she really *had* been in; the slave market, the battles, the insane teacher and alternate future where he hadn't even known her. If only he knew.

"No! I'm fine now. I—I was just wondering if maybe...you'd come visit this weekend. So we can talk about...stuff."

"I'm not taking you out of school, Kristine. You've got to straighten up and do better."

"Oh, Dad. It's nothing like that. I don't want to come home— well, I mean, I do—but school's OK now. I really want to talk about you and—and Mom." Her throat tightened, but she pushed out the words she'd been waiting so long to say. "You're being selfish. You should go home. Talk to her, at least. We both know that."

He sighed. "We've discussed this, Kristine. Your mother and I think—"

"No, Dad. *You* think for once. All Mom does is cry—I've heard her. You always tell *me* to do what's right. Well, I'm ready. I'm going to try harder here. Even be good! I'm going to make my family proud."

He let out a long breath. "Kristine, I am proud of you. I always have been. You know that."

"Then make me proud of *you* again."

He was silent.

"Will you at least come talk to me this weekend? Please?"

"No," he finally said.

Her heart dropped. "But—"

"I'll be there in an hour," he said. "And we'll talk."

Kristi smiled when she hung up. It didn't mean that her parents were going to get back together, after all. But it was a start.

EPILOGUE

The night before Kristi was to leave GW Prep for winter break, she lay in her room in the girls' dorm, watching the lump of blankets that covered her roommate rise and fall in the green glow of the alarm clock. It was 12:44 AM. Her roommate's breaths were slow and even. At last, Kristi pushed her own covers off and opened their door a crack. The long hallway was dim and empty. She crept out and stole down the steps like a jewel thief, careful to muffle her slippered footfalls. At the bottom, she moved past the door marked *EXIT* and went on into the computer lab. Five red dots marked the computers softly humming in the dark. She sat at the one furthest from the door, cringing when the chair creaked. She clicked the mouse and the screen burst to life, bathing the room in a pale glow. She clicked the *Grades* icon and typed her login, *soccergirl,* and password, *Ty1780.* Her finals had been posted, all A's. Even in history. *Especially* in history. She opened Google search and typed *Xavier Arnold.*

Xavier Arnold, (???—August 3, 1815) was a British spy during the Revolutionary War. He was captured near Tarrytown, NY and accused of conspiring with his alleged cousin Benedict Arnold to turn West Point over to British soldiers. Due to his strange ravings at trial, he was declared insane and spared the gallows.

After the war, Xavier was transported to England where he was later arrested for harassing Benedict Arnold. During a second trial, he claimed to be Benedict Arnold's great-great-great-great-great-great grandson. Xavier Arnold lived out the rest of his days in Bedlam Asylum in London.

She smiled, then took a deep breath and typed *Ty Jordan.*

The Jordan brothers, Ty (???—July 4, 1865) and Thomas (???—July 7, 1865) helped revolutionize early nineteenth century medicine and agriculture in America. They are also credited with being two of America's earliest abolitionists.

After graduating from Pennsylvania University Medical School in 1792, Ty and Thomas Jordan traveled through the young American country, working in hospitals and clinics, introducing medical and surgical techniques that saved thousands of lives. They donated most of their earnings to anti-slavery causes. Neither married, but they jointly adopted ten orphaned boys and girls, including five freed slaves. Through their lifetimes, they bought and freed an estimated 128 African slaves. Their adopted children and grandchildren continued their work, providing safe havens for escaped slaves traveling the Underground Railroad through Pennsylvania, Maryland, and Virginia.

In 1862, the Jordan brothers were summoned to a private meeting with President Abraham Lincoln. A week later, Lincoln announced he would sign the

Emancipation Proclamation, freeing all slaves in the Union.

Ty and Thomas Jordan died peacefully, a few days apart, on their Pennsylvania farm in 1865, surrounded by their many adopted children, grandchildren, and great-grandchildren. Their Pennsylvanian home, a famed station along the Underground Railroad, is now a historical site and museum.

***

Long, deep brown fields of freshly turned earth sat beneath the glaring sun. Ty pulled off his wide-trimmed hat and wiped sweat from his brow. The early May morning was hotter than he thought it should be. So humid, as if the air itself was sweating. It was going to be a *long* summer. He leaned on his hoe, breathed in the spring air, a mixture of sweet white violets and the earthy horse manure they used as fertilizer.

Thomas stood on the other side of the field, hat off, leaning on his hoe as well. As they smiled across at each other, Miss Martha rang the triangle from the porch, calling them in to supper.

They had a stare-down competition. Suddenly Ty grinned. They dropped their hoes at the same time and raced each other back to the farmhouse, laughing all the way.

THE END

Watch out....

...for Kristi and Ty's next adventure as they elude slave catchers along the Underground Railroad. TIME UNDERGROUND will be the second in the American Epochs series of time-travel adventures. Coming soon from Northampton House!

ABOUT THE AUTHOR

Todd McClimans is an elementary school principal and former fifth grade teacher. He holds BA degrees in Creative Writing and Elementary Education and master's degrees in Creative writing and Educational Leadership.

Todd lives in Pennsylvania with his wife and three kids. A self-styled history buff and fantasy nerd, he first became interested in writing about American history when teaching his fifth graders the riveting stories of patriots and their struggle for independence during the Revolutionary War. He aims to bring history to life for young readers by writing stories with a careful mixture of historical fact and fantastical story-telling with characters to which readers can relate.

Outside of his duties as principal, husband, father, and writer, Todd spends his free time (as sparse as it may be) reading, running, and riding his bike. He's an avid reader of anything fantasy and lists his current favorite authors (a list that is never exhaustive) as Lois Lowry, J.K. Rowlings, J.R.R. Tolkien, Stephen King, David McCollough, and George R.R. Martin. TIME TRAITOR is his first published novel.

ABOUT NORTHAMPTON HOUSE PRESS

Northampton House publishes carefully chosen fiction, poetry, and selected nonfiction. Our logo represents the Greek muse Polyhymnnia. Our mission is to discover great new writers and give them a chance to springboard into fame. Our watchword is quality, not quantity. Watch the Northampton House list at www.northampton-house.com,, and Like us on Facebook – "Northampton House Press" – to discover more innovative works from brilliant new writers.

1/16 ∅

CPSIA information can be obtained at www.ICGtesting.com
Printed in the USA
LVOW11s1738250614

391685LV00007B/940/P

9 781937 997366